KU-215-041

Nightmares 3

This Armada book belongs to:

_____

_____

_____

Other Spinechillers in Armada

Armada Ghost Books Nos. 1–15
edited by Christine Bernard and Mary Danby

Nightmares
Nightmares 2
edited by Mary Danby

Black Harvest
The Beggar's Curse
The Witch of Lagg
by Ann Cheetham

The Monster Trap & Other True Mysteries
The Restless Bones & Other True Mysteries
The Hell Hound & Other True Mysteries
The Screaming Skull & Other True Mysteries
The Vampire Terror & Other True Mysteries
by Peter Haining

Hardy Boys Ghost Stories
by Franklin W. Dixon

Nightmares 3

Edited by Mary Danby
Illustrated by John Higgins

An Armada Original

Nightmares 3 was first published in Armada
in 1985 by Fontana Paperbacks,
8 Grafton Street, London W1X 3LA.

Armada is an imprint of Fontana Paperbacks,
a division of the Collins Publishing Group.

Printed in Great Britain by
Williams Collins Sons & Co. Ltd., Glasgow

CONTENTS

ACKNOWLEDGEMENTS

The Editor gratefully acknowledges permission to use copyright material to the following:

Antony Bennett for *Clifftops*.
Copyright © Antony Bennett 1985.

Johnny Yen for *Barnacles*.
Copyright © Johnny Yen 1985.

Alan W. Lear for *Dead Letter*.
Copyright © Alan W. Lear 1985.

Sydney J. Bounds for *House of Horror*.
Copyright © Sydney J. Bounds 1985.

Samantha Lee for *The Diary*.
Copyright © Samantha Lee 1985.

Roger Malisson for *Shadow of the Rope*.
Copyright © Roger Malisson 1985.

Brian Mooney for *Joplin's*.
Copyright © Brian Mooney 1985.

Phillip C. Heath for *The Shaft*.
Copyright © Phillip C. Heath 1985.

Old Wiggie is copyright © Mary Danby 1985.

CLIFFTOPS

Antony Bennett

CLIFFTOPS had been designed by a lunatic, or so Jonathan's father always said. Jonathan had to agree. Nothing about the hotel's construction seemed sane: no room was the twin of any other, no two walls ran quite parallel, and the long, strangely twisted corridors were often interrupted by a short flight of stairs, which made it difficult to keep track of which floor you were on, and caused many of the guests to become hopelessly lost.

Jonathan never got lost. He could find his way around Clifftops with a blindfold on. The hotel had been his home since he was nine, and over the years he had grown to love its many peculiarities.

"Jon?" his father called from downstairs. "Where are you?"

"Up here." He was in one of the big rooms on the third floor, throwing dust-sheets over the elderly furniture. Glad to leave his work for a while, he went out into the corridor and leaned over the mahogany banisters. "What is it?" he yelled down the stairwell.

"Your mother and I are off to visit Aunt Emily. Are you sure you don't want to come?"

"I'm sure," he said.

Visits to Aunt Emily always turned out the same way. She would smile and say something polite about how tall he had grown, and then invariably serve extra-strong tea and soft biscuits. He would be bored within minutes.

7

He had decided that it would be preferable to stay behind and get on with some work.

"It'll be dark by the time we get back," said his father. "Will you be all right in here on your own?"

"Of course I will. I can look after myself."

"I know. But I'm going to lock the door, just in case. I don't want any intruders sneaking in while you're busy up there."

Jonathan shrugged. "O.K. If it makes you feel better."

For the first time that he could recall, Jonathan was all alone inside Clifftops. Apart from the cries of the wheeling seagulls the huge building was perfectly quiet: even the constant pounding of the waves seemed hushed. The last of the guests had packed their belongings and gone home. The small complement of staff had done likewise. The summer season was at an end, and now the hotel was being shut down for the duration of the winter.

Without people to give it life, the grand old place became just a pocket of empty stillness, and Jonathan soon felt dwarfed within its majestic interior. All of the ceilings were unfashionably high, and the rooms were more generous than any modern hotel could offer.

He went back to the dust-sheets and continued to drape them over the furniture.

When the room was finished he leaned out of the window and closed the wooden shutters. From outside, it looked as though the hotel's many eyes were being closed, one by one. Finally, he locked the door with one of a bunch of brass keys.

Another room done; how many more to go?

It would take several more days to close the place down completely—to lock the doors, cover the furniture, sweep the floors, and drain all of the water pipes to prevent them from bursting in the middle of the winter. When everything was done, Jonathan and his parents would leave the hotel to go and live in a small house that they owned in the town. It felt cramped compared to Clifftops, but at least it was peaceful. They had nobody to think about but themselves, and that made a pleasant change.

Jonathan had to attend to all of the rooms on the third floor—all except one. Room 313. He would never go into room 313. No way. That was the room where Mervyn Ridley had died.

Poor Mervyn Ridley.

No one had taken much notice of him when he had booked in during the summer. He had been a pleasant, unassuming man—" . . . a real gentleman," as someone had put it afterwards—who minded his own business and spoke to barely a soul. His white hair was always neatly combed, and he carried an elegant walking cane which had a handle shaped like a hooded cobra. Even though he had been old, no one had suspected that he might die — and yet, while he slept, in the deepest, darkest, stillest part of the night, his weak heart had simply collapsed.

A shiver passed through Jonathan. He had not entered room 313 since, fearing that some terrible remnant of death might linger there.

Just as he was letting himself into the next room, the phone rang downstairs.

Leaving the keys in the door, he jogged down the six flights of stairs into Reception, where the ringing created a jangling echo in the stillness. Breathless, and cursing the fact that his father had turned off the lift, he leaned across the receptionist's desk—and the instant before his fingers touched the receiver, the phone fell silent.

He groaned.

It had been one of those days.

9

The ground floor of Clifftops was unusually gloomy. Two days ago, all of the shutters had been closed and padlocked against the harsh winter storms that would blow in off the sea.

Just as he was about to go back upstairs, he heard a noise that made him freeze.

He looked across the reception area, through the archway that led into the darkened dining-room. The unmistakable sound of footsteps came from in there: light and swift, like those of a child.

His father's parting words ran through his mind. *"I'm going to lock the door, just in case. I don't want any intruders sneaking in . . ."* He wondered how anybody could have got in—the hotel was locked up tighter than Fort Knox.

He went quietly to the archway and stood there for a moment, staring into the darkness. There was nothing to see. It gradually dawned on him that the footsteps came not from the dining-room, but from the adjoining kitchen. It sounded as though someone was running about on the tiled floor.

Gathering courage, he walked cautiously between the empty tables, his eyes slowly growing accustomed to the gloom. The swing doors which led into the kitchen had small glass portholes in them, and he could see that the kitchen was also in darkness. Nervously, he went up to one of the portholes and peered through—and he was amazed at what he saw.

It was a little girl, no older than five or six. She was happily running amongst the shadows, holding out her arms like the wings of a bird in flight. She was so absorbed in her game that she totally failed to notice Jonathan's arrival, and he was able to watch her, spellbound, for quite a time. There was something odd about her, something distinctly old-fashioned. Her dusty hair was set in ringlets that bounced as she ran, her skin was pale, untouched by the sun, and she wore a threadbare dress that was cobweb grey. Only her lips, small and cherry pink, seemed possessed of any colour.

Jonathan gently pushed the door open and went into the kitchen. He made no sound, and the little girl continued to play, oblivious to his presence. He hardly dared to take his eyes off her. His fingers reached across the wall by his side, searching for the lights. At last he discovered the switches. He threw them all—and could not have been more surprised at the girl's reaction to the sudden blaze of light. She screamed, as if in pain. Her hands flew up to protect her eyes, and, apparently blinded, she ran into the side of a stove in a frantic bid to escape.

"It's all right," said Jonathan, distressed to have caused such panic, "I'm not going to hurt you . . . "

She wailed, and ran across the kitchen towards the small door that led into the wine cellar.

"Hey! Come back! Who are you?"

He chased after her.

The wine cellar was also in darkness, and as soon as he reached the top of the steps he switched on the lights. He saw the little girl disappearing between the ancient racks of dust-laden bottles, and he hurried down the steps after her.

The cellar was enormous; it sprawled beneath the entirety of the huge hotel, and nowadays only a small proportion of it was still in use. Much of it was affected by damp. The little girl made straight for the unused area, where the lights did not reach and forgotten junk was kept in untidy heaps. Jonathan stumbled over the rubbish as he followed her into the deepening gloom.

She went further into the cellar than he had ever been.

11

"Come back!" he called, but she ignored him.

Suddenly, she seemed to disappear into the ground — unless his eyes had deceived him, she had lowered herself into a deep hole—and then a great trap door swung over and slammed shut on top of her.

He got hold of the biggest torch that he could find in the hotel. Against his every rational instinct, he was going to follow her. He had to find out who she was, and what she was doing inside his home. He could have waited for his parents, of course, or even have contacted the police, but that seemed a little rash. *After all,* he thought, *she's only a little girl.* He was perfectly able to cope. And he knew his parents would be proud when they found out how well he had handled things in their absence.

Armed with the torch's powerful light, he went back down into the cellar. Slowly and cautiously he picked his way amongst the junk towards the trap door. It proved more difficult to find than he had imagined; the wood was so old and rotten that it had adopted the colour of the stone floor around it. Only the rusted hinges gave away its presence.

It yawned open with surprising ease, almost as though oil had recently been applied, and a steep flight of stone steps was revealed beneath.

He was not apprehensive—at least, not at first, not until he started to go down the steps, and then genuine fear took root. Gone was the warm, familiar side of the hotel he thought he knew so well, and revealed was another, less pleasant side to its character. Darkness and dampness overwhelmed him. A chill, foul draught touched his face.

The torch, which had seemed so powerful at first, was hardly able to penetrate the intense darkness. The damp stone walls on either side of him were barely wide enough apart to accept his shoulders, and the steps were slippery and crooked. He trod with caution.

The further down he went, the colder it got. His breath escaped as mist.

He half expected a spider's web to brush against his face, but none did, which suggested that the steps were often used.

A sudden noise made him stop.

He listened, and his heart lurched and began to thump heavily as he heard something scratching and scuffling about in the dark. Whatever it was, it was on the steps just behind him. He turned slowly, and directed the torch towards the source of the disturbance—and what he saw made him catch his breath in shock.

It was a rat.

Huge and bristling, it arched its back and stared defiantly into the torchlight with its tiny black eyes. Its whiskers quivered. An icy shudder rushed up Jonathan's spine. He had walked right past the rat without even noticing. He must have come within an inch of treading on it.

Part of him desperately wanted to dash back up the steps and out into the light, but he would not allow himself to do so. The little girl had passed this way without fear, and his pride would be hurt if he admitted to being more afraid than her. So he forced himself to go on; deeper and deeper. And the air grew stale and became unpleasant to breathe.

At one point, he almost came to grief. His foot slipped, his ankle gave way, and he only just managed to prevent himself from falling by slamming his hands against the walls. The torch nearly went flying. "Easy," he whispered to himself, "just take it easy."

He was beginning to suspect that the steps would

descend forever, when they finally came to an end. The walls widened beyond his reach, and the torchlight revealed a scene that simply took his breath away.

He found himself inside an enormous cavern, the like of which he had never seen before. Water dripped, and echoed. Wherever he pointed the torch he found something new to awe him. High above, stalactites were poised like daggers; they appeared to move as the torchlight played across them. Some had reached the ground to form natural pillars, giving the place a cathedral-like air.

He knew that the cliffs were riddled with caverns, but he had never suspected that one as impressive as this lay beneath his own home, and he was astonished to have made such a discovery.

For a while his fear had been forgotten, but it was quickly re-awakened when he heard something move behind him. He swung around, fully expecting to see another rat. Instead, the torch revealed an old man, who squinted in the glare. "Please . . ." The man shielded his eyes. "The light is painful."

Jonathan backed away, dumbstruck. His foot hit a rock, he stumbled and fell. He dropped the torch, and it broke against the ground and went out. His startled gasp echoed around the darkened cavern.

"Don't worry," said the old man. "There's light enough to see by, even without the aid of your electric toy. We lit all the candles when little Alice said you were coming. We have no real need of them ourselves; our eyes are particularly keen in the dark."

And Jonathan realised that the cavern was indeed lit by candles; about a dozen of them were spaced out around the walls. They flickered, and created leaping shadows.

The old man approached him. "You didn't hurt

yourself, did you? I didn't mean to frighten you like that. Here—let me help you up."

"Keep away from me!" Jonathan hurried to his feet.

"Relax, my friend, relax. Surely, you're not afraid. Look at me. I'm old and feeble: you're a strong young man. What harm could I possibly do you?"

"I don't know. Just keep away from me." He noticed that the old man used a cane to help him walk, and he suddenly realised how foolish his actions must have appeared. He tried to control his fear and regain his composure. "Who are you?" he asked.

The old man offered his long, thin hand to shake. "My name is Mervyn Ridley."

Jonathan's heart shrank to the size of a small stone; shock drank the blood from his cheeks. The man before him was horribly familiar now: his walking-cane had a handle shaped like a hooded cobra. "You're *dead*!" The words jerked out without thought. "You died in room 313! You—you can't . . . "

Mervyn Ridley gave a ghastly smile. "My dear friend, take my word for it, I'm not dead. Here—shake my hand; feel the firmness of my flesh if you need proof that I'm no ghost."

"It can't be true . . . " He started to back away.

"Don't go." Mervyn Ridley quickly grabbed Jonathan's shoulders. His fingers felt like steel hooks, his skin was dry and white. "I want you to stay. We all want you to stay."

"All?"

"There are many of us here, and our numbers are growing all the time." He pulled Jonathan closer, his eyes narrowed. "You can join us, my friend. You can become one of us."

Jonathan thought he heard somebody whispering in the

shadows—or perhaps it was a draught sighing through the rocks; perhaps it was just his imagination.

"You might recognise one or two more of my companions," Mervyn Ridley continued. "Remember the maid who only worked in Clifftops for a week and then never came back? She's down here. She joined us gladly. And there are others—people from the town, and holiday-makers who decided to stay with us rather than go home."

"I—I don't understand."

"You will, shortly." He turned to one side. "Alice? Come here and introduce yourself to our new friend."

The old man let Jonathan go. He looked around. The little girl came out of the dark cranny where she had been hiding and walked quietly towards him, her head bowed. Then she curtsied. "Pleased to make your acquaintance," she said.

Jonathan was totally bewildered. He felt as if he was caught in some incredible dream where nothing quite made sense. He turned to Mervyn Ridley, hoping to get some information out of him. "Those steps and the trap door back there," he said. "Did you make them?"

He shook his head. "You saw for yourself how old they are. They were here long before we arrived." He pointed towards the rear of the cavern. "There are some more steps over there; they lead into a tunnel that collapsed long ago. It's quite impassable now, but from what I can tell, it used to lead all the way down to the beach. If you ask me, this cavern was used by smugglers in times gone by. It must have been the ideal place for hiding contraband."

"How did you find out about it?"

"Ah . . . now, my friend, that would be telling. We have ways and means that are totally beyond your comprehension."

16

It was clear that the old man intended to give nothing away, and Jonathan could come up with no rational explanation for anything that he had seen. Mervyn Ridley had been pronounced dead by a doctor, and yet here he was, still very much alive. That alone was mysterious enough—but what was he doing here with all these other people? Why did they need to live like hermits? And how could they have survived under a busy hotel without being found out until now?

Nothing made sense.

"Your mind is filled with turmoil," said Mervyn Ridley with a wry smile. "Very well, my friend; if your thirst for knowledge is so great, you shall learn the truth. But be warned—you might find that the truth has a bitter taste."

Alice glanced up. "Please," she begged the old man, "let me be the one to tell him. It's been so long . . ."

He nodded. "Be my guest."

As she approached, Jonathan was struck by how small and delicate she appeared. She was so pale, and she looked so cold. Perhaps she was sick. Perhaps the old man was keeping her here against her will . . . It was certainly possible.

Her face was hidden in shadow. "You'll have to bend down," she said softly. "I want to whisper."

Jonathan fancied he caught a hint of desperation in her voice.

He leaned forward.

She placed her small hand on his shoulder.

When her head approached his, he was half expecting her to make a whispered plea for help. Instead, she lashed out like a snake and bit into his neck, chewing the tendons and sucking, sucking. He screamed in agony and knocked her away with his fists, and as she fell her needle sharp teeth ripped across his neck, and blood splashed down his

Alice licked her lips . . .

shirt. His throat burned like fire; he pressed his hand over the wound to stem the bleeding.

Alice cowered on the ground and hissed furiously. Her eyes blazed. Her bloodied mouth was open, exposing a pair of pointed white fangs.

"You'll have to forgive little Alice," said Mervyn Ridley, calmly. "She tends to be rather clumsy with her victims. She's so excitable."

Jonathan felt sick and suddenly dizzy. The cavern seemed to roll and sway. Mervyn Ridley grinned at him and displayed his deadly vampire fangs. Alice licked her lips.

In sheer panic he fled, and the speed of his departure took them both by surprise. Alice leapt after him, but she was not quick enough—her fingertips only brushed Jonathan's heels as he vanished up the stone steps two at a time, knocking his elbows, crashing his shins, too numb to feel the pain.

"There's nowhere you can run that we can't find you!" yelled Mervyn Ridley.

It took an eternity to climb the steps, and when he got to the top his thighs and lungs screamed from the effort, but he only paused long enough to slam the trap door shut. He ran blindly through the darkened section of the cellar, tripping and stumbling, until at last he reached the part that was brightly lit.

A moment later he had mounted the cellar steps and was back in the kitchen, with the door shut firmly behind him.

He trembled uncontrollably.

There was no doubt in his mind that they were following him; several times on the steps he thought he had felt Alice's hungry breath on the back of his neck. He had to act quickly. The key to the cellar door was kept in a drawer in one of the kitchen units. Thankfully, he found it without having to rummage. He jammed it into the keyhole, and the lock gave a satisfying clack as he turned it. There was no other way out. They were trapped.

He tried to deny the weakness that sapped his soul and made lead of his limbs—now more than ever he needed his strength—but even if the shock and the blood loss had left him unaffected, he still would have been unsure what to do next.

From the darkest recesses of his memory, vague images from old horror films drifted before his mind's eye—fangs and bats and blood; silk-lined coffins laced with dusty cobwebs; vampires with stakes hammered deep into their chests . . . He shuddered.

Then came the moment that he had been dreading.

He held his breath, and stared at the door handle.

It was turning, slowly.

"No . . ."

It rattled as Mervyn Ridley tried to force the lock.

Please, he thought, *don't let him get out.*

The old man's voice boomed from inside the cellar. "You underestimate me!"

There was a long, silent pause.

Then Jonathan became aware of a curious sensation. It felt as if the air around him was vibrating. His skin tingled. He sensed that something dreadful was building up —something powerful was about to be unleashed.

Almost imperceptibly, the cellar door began to tremble. As he watched, the shaking gradually intensified. The key jangled in the lock. Suddenly, the door was dealt a thunderous blow; it nearly burst off its hinges, and Jonathan backed away in shock. The entire door had bulged and almost split in half. The shuddering grew even more violent; then it was struck again, and this time the wood splintered. It was breaking apart. The old man was using some nightmarish force to batter his way out, and there was nothing Jonathan could do to stop him.

He fled.

His first thought was to escape through the front door, but horror clutched his heart at the last moment. The front door was locked, and he had left his keys upstairs. In desperation he tried to break the door open, but it would not give. He was getting weaker by the minute.

The cellar door burst off its hinges.

Acting purely on instinct, Jonathan ran up the stairs. Out of the corner of his eye he saw Mervyn Ridley hurrying after him, and he panicked and ran faster than he had ever done before. He was convinced that he would be caught at any moment.

He got all the way up to the third floor before he realised that Mervyn Ridley was no longer behind him. He clasped his side and doubled up in pain as a stitch gnawed into his abdomen; he was breathing hard and fast. The wound in his neck was stinging badly, as if an infection was festering there.

Silence surrounded him.

He was alone.

Apparently, the old man had given up the chase—but, surely, there would have to be a good reason for him doing that. Something had prevented him from coming up the stairs. And then Jonathan realised what it was.

Sunlight. Pure and simple sunlight. Its touch was fatal to vampires. On the ground floor all of the shutters were closed, but up here most of them were still open, and the sun shone in without restraint. For the moment, he was safe.

"You are a fool!" Mervyn Ridley bellowed from downstairs. "You've run yourself into a trap up there.

There's no escape for you now. Barely half an hour from now the sun will have set, and then, my friend, you will be mine!"

Jonathan looked out of the window. The sun was drifting towards the horizon, and the sky was turning pink. There was no time to lose.

He sat on the floor, leaning against the wall of the corridor, his knees hugged against his chest for comfort. The sun had gone down twenty minutes ago, but the hotel was not in darkness. He had seen to that. Every light on the third floor was switched on, and all of the lampshades had been removed to give maximum glare. Of course, the blaze of light would do no real harm—only sunlight could do that—but it would at least hurt their eyes, and that would give him a slight advantage.

The phones were all dead. He had attempted to ring the police, but the vampire had been one step ahead of him. He guessed that the line had been cut.

Why was he taking so long to come?

The waiting was the worst part of all.

Jonathan's fingers clutched a small, silver crucifix that he had found in one of the rooms; he hoped it would afford him some protection. If it failed, then there was only one course of action left open to him. At his feet lay a wooden stake—or what he hoped would pass for a wooden stake. He had broken the handle off a broom by trapping it in a doorway and using leverage to make it snap. One end of the splintered handle was jagged now, and sharp enough to pierce anybody's heart. All he needed was the courage to use it.

The slow minutes passed. And still, nothing occurred.

He imagined that Mervyn Ridley was relishing the predicament that he was in. He wished something would happen. He wanted it all to be over.

The wound on his neck was dry and sore now, but he had lost much blood before it had healed. He felt cold and weak, and his breath came in odd gasps. What little strength he retained, he intended to save for his final struggle against the vampire.

Tap . . . tap . . . tap . . .

His thoughts were disturbed by the noise which came up the stairs.

Tap . . . tap . . .

It was caused by a walking cane, and he knew before he looked that it was a cane with a handle shaped like a hooded cobra.

His heart thundered.

He took hold of the broken broom handle, and with its assistance he slowly pushed himself up to his feet.

Mervyn Ridley appeared at the top of the stairs and walked towards Jonathan with calm assurance. "Well, well," he said, "what do we have here? Like frightened prey you've run yourself into a dead end." He smiled. "And so the predator closes in . . ."

"Stay away from me!" said Jonathan, holding out the crucifix. It shone in the light.

Mervyn Ridley arched an eyebrow. "Such impudence. Your bravery is touching, my friend, but that silver trinket will do you no good. Oh, it's repulsive enough, but, I promise you, it'll take more than that to stop me."

Unexpectedly, the old man reached out and grabbed Jonathan's wrist. His strength was frightening. He squeezed so tightly that Jonathan thought his bones would crack. "Drop the crucifix," he snarled. "Drop it now, or I'll break your arm." The crucifix trembled in Jonathan's fingers. He held on until the last possible moment, until the pain grew too intense, and then he let it drop.

"Good," said Mervyn Ridley as he kicked it out of the

way. He grinned, and showed his fangs. "You learn quickly. I like that."

Jonathan held up the broken broom handle and pointed it like a spear.

"Now what? A stick? Do you intend to kill me with a stick?"

"I can do it."

"Oh, I don't doubt you can. But you won't."

"What makes you so sure?"

"Because, my friend, you would be killing one of your own kind."

"What . . ?"

"Oh, yes." Mervyn Ridley's eyes gleamed. "You see, the bite that little Alice gave you may only have been a scratch, but it was more than enough to do the trick. Even as we speak, your heart is dying. Can't you feel it? It's getting weaker by the minute—slower . . . and slower . . . Before this night is through, it will fail and die like a rotted husk. And then, my friend, you will rise again as a superior being—as one of the glorious undead. Like us, you will discover the heady delight of feasting upon human blood."

"*No!*"

Sudden rage boiled within him.

He gritted his teeth and thrust the sharp end of the broom handle into Mervyn Ridley's chest. The old man had no time to think. He gave a loud gasp and staggered backwards, and Jonathan pushed as hard as he could—but the broom handle went in all wrong; it got jammed between the old man's ribs, and Jonathan lacked the necessary strength to force it all the way in. "Oh, no . . . please . . . " He had never imagined that he might fail in such a way. He grimaced and tried to throw his weight behind the handle, all to no avail. The vampire's blood was dark and plentiful, but it came out of his veins and not his heart.

He knocked Jonathan cruelly aside, and plucked the broom handle out of his chest as if it were nothing more annoying than a splinter. He hurled it over the banisters and sent it clattering down the stairs. An ordinary man would have been felled by such an attack, but Mervyn Ridley was apparently unaffected.

There were tears in Jonathan's eyes. He had collapsed, and lay on the floor, totally exhausted. His last ounce of strength had been spent. It hurt to breathe, and his neck had started to bleed again. His heart pounded strangely, without rhythm. "I hate you," he murmured. "I hate you."

Mervyn Ridley towered over him and looked down into his eyes. "You'll grow to love me," he said. "Believe me, you're a very fortunate young man. Do you understand the importance of what is happening to you? As one of the undead you will live forever. Consider that. The passing years will not touch you: youth is yours for all eternity. You will develp physical strength beyond your wildest imaginings, and you will acquire senses that you never even knew existed. Many doors have opened to you tonight."

Jonathan's eyelids flickered. Everything became blurred and went into a spin. "I won't . . . join you . . . "

"You have no choice." Mervyn Ridley knelt down and lifted him into his strong arms. He touched Jonathan's neck with his cool fingers, and seemed delighted with the blood that he found there. He licked his lips hungrily. "Here . . . " He leaned forward and bared his fangs. "Let me help you on your way."

Jonathan sat alone on the stairs.

Clifftops was in darkness. He had switched off all the lights, and then systematically smashed every single light bulb in the place. Darkness suited his mood.

Soon, he thought, *soon*.

A car turned into the drive, and an uncontrollable thrill rushed through him. At last, they were home. He ran down the stairs and went to the front door. He had to shield his eyes when the painfully bright headlights shone through the small pane of frosted glass.

Shortly, it would all be over. His last links with the mortal world would be severed forever, and he could begin his new existence afresh.

He went to greet them, adjusting the collar of his clean shirt to ensure it hid the puncture marks on his neck.

As the door opened, and his mother's hand reached for the light switch that wouldn't work, he gave a small smile, and eagerly licked his ruby red lips.

BARNACLES

Johnny Yen

THE ACORN BARNACLES is one of the most common of sea creatures. A mile-long stretch of rocky shore may contain as many as two thousand million of them. So if Gary crushed some with his boots, or dashed some more with a rock, it hardly constituted a serious threat to the local marine ecology.

Even so, there was no excuse for the wanton destruction of the harmless crustaceans that gathered in and around the rock-pools where Gary was searching for winkles. It was not their fault that Gary had not found as many winkles as he expected. And they were certainly not to blame when he slipped and fell on the greasy seaweed, and was nipped by a crab.

The sensible crab scuttled off sideways. But the barnacles remained where they were, and so were cracked open and flattened simply because they were there. The fewer winkles Gary found, the more barnacles were smashed and split by stones and boots. It was not a good day for barnacles.

"Have you got many yet?" Gary heard his father call from across the beach.

"No, not really," Gary said reluctantly. "There aren't many about."

"You can't be looking properly," his father replied, coming over to him. "I've got loads. Look—" He held up a plastic bag bulging with winkles.

"Yeah, but you told me only to get big ones," Gary protested. "All I've seen so far is tiny ones."

"Rubbish," his father said, laughing. "Get on with it, you lazy devil. I want that bag filled."

"You're joking!" exclaimed Gary. "That's miles too much. We'll never get through that many."

"No it isn't," said his father. "They've got to go round the whole family, don't forget."

"That's still too many. There's only you and Nan that really like 'em."

"Well, those we don't eat we'll put in the freezer, won't we, dopey," said his father somewhat impatiently.

Gary groaned. "But I can't find hardly any," he whined. "I'll never fill this bag."

"Oh, get on with it and stop moaning," retorted his father, turning away from him and resuming the search.

Gary sighed. Shielding his eyes from the summer sun, he admired the view again. He had been coming to Flamborough Head with his father to get winkles once or twice a year for as long as he could remember, but he never tired of the place. It was always one of the high-points of his annual holiday with his relatives in Yorkshire, though he had long since lost the taste for winkles.

The process of collecting and eating winkles could be quite a chore. The long car journey from Hull was interesting, but actually searching for the little sea-water snails soon became boring. It had pleased him more when he was younger, perhaps because he had not then been expected to work so hard at it.

Only after the winkles had been boiled were they edible. Gary could eat winkles all evening without feeling full only because it took him so long to remove each creature from its shell. He had never mastered the subtle art of winkle-picking, and usually managed to skewer only the rubbery end of the winkle with his pin, leaving the sweet, succulent tail behind.

Negotiating the cliffs of Flamborough Head made winkling worthwhile, though. Even with a rope it could be quite hazardous, but Gary enjoyed it immensely. The rocky coastline was twisted and uneven. The towering chalk and clay cliffs were crumbling at the top and undermined by shallow caves and numerous rabbit warrens. Craggy arches of soft rock stood apart from the main cliff-face like lonely windows on to the slippery **flat** rock beach and the placid sea beyond.

Much of the beach was now clothed in seaweed, which seemed to Gary to become thicker and slimier each year. There was only a small area completely free of it. This was the narrow margin at the base of the cliff, which consisted of smooth clean white stones of varying sizes.

Gary wondered vaguely which pool he should try next. He did not expect to fill his bag now, but wanted to collect just enough to make his haul not look paltry beside his father's, before he went for a swim.

Part of the reason for Gary's lack of success as a winkler was because he couldn't be bothered. But—in the pools he had searched, at least—there were indeed fewer decent-sized winkles about than usual.

Mostly all he found were barnacles. He came across two more small crabs, a number of squat brown unpleasant-looking sea-anemones, and many staunch grey limpets. But barnacles outnumbered everything else.

At first they annoyed him by being everywhere. He soon began to enjoy their presence, though, as they were easy prey. Collecting winkles was dull enough, but not finding any was even worse. Killing barnacles was considerably more amusing then either. Crabs moved too quickly to be crushed. Limpets were usually too strong and sturdy. He did not like to touch the sea-anemones for fear of being stung. So the barnacles took the full brunt of his destructive boredom.

Their bodies smashed easily with a satisfying *shick* as he brought down heavy stones upon their clustered communities.

Crustaceans, even more than insects, suffer silently. Their obliteration, then, is quite easy to bear for their executioners, who do not think of them as suffering animals.

The barnacles accepted their fate stoically. They did not recoil from the pain like worms or slugs; nor did their four valves open out and palpitate in mortal terror. So Gary mashed, squashed and crushed them in their hundreds, until they were just a grey-brown sticky pulp, clinging wetly to the edges of the rock-pools, slicked and slimy with their own life-fluids.

Gary had collected only twenty or so more winkles by then, but he wanted to swim.

After wiping the squashed barnacles from the soles of his boots with some seaweed, he skipped nimbly over the rocks towards his father, being careful this time not to slip.

He noted with disappointment that the plastic bag his father held was even more swollen.

"Is that all you've got?" his father exclaimed with surprise.

"All there is is little ones," Gary repeated with less conviction than before.

"You're just idle, Gary, that's all," said his father.

"Coming for a swim?" Gary said, ignoring him.

"Haven't got my swimming costume, have I, you daft devil."

"I'll go on my own, then. Here, take these." He handed over the winkles he had found.

"What about a towel?" said his father as Gary made his way towards the dry white pebbles.

"There's one in the car, isn't there?"

"I suppose so. Don't be long, will you? Your grandmother will be wondering where we are."

"O.K."

Gary wore trunks under his ragged denim shorts, so he was soon ready to face the sea, leaving his clothes by the edge of the cliff.

The tide was a long way out, and the deep water further still. It was a slow journey. The layers of ropy seaweed tangled round his ankles and toes, making his footing awkward. The sea-bed was pitted and lumpy. Where it jutted through the seaweed, jagged protrusions grazed Gary's feet. So, too, did the rough shells of the underwater barnacles, now that he had neither the weight nor the footwear with which to flatten them.

Gary turned to see how far he had come. The bulky, blue T-shirted figure of his father was now a mere speck. The water was barely over his knees. He must make faster progress than this or he would have to turn back before he had a chance to swim.

He tried to move more quickly. Walking through water is not easy, though, and he soon stumbled. The seaweed became still more dense. It clung to his legs under the water and he could not shake it off. His shins felt coated in it.

Carefully steadying himself he lifted a leg from the water to remove the annoying seaweed.

He found that it was not seaweed on his legs at all, but barnacles. He nearly fell over with surprise.

Gary did not know much about marine biology, but he

was sure that barnacles—the varieties common to the shores of England, at any rate—remained stationary for most of their lives; their bony shells were normally cemented firmly to rocks or groynes, he thought.

He tried to prise the rogue barnacles from his shins with his fingernails, but they held on grimly.

Sighing, he continued his trek into the sea. He would have to wait until he got back to the beach before he could remove the stubborn creatures; there he would be able to use more force against them. A few barnacles adhering to his legs might annoy him, but they would not prevent him from swimming.

By the time the water had reached the tops of his thighs, though, the barnacles were an inch thick from there to his toes. It was beyond a joke, and he realised that he must return to the beach.

But by now any movement was difficult, for the burden of barnacles was becoming increasingly heavy. He could hardly bend his knees. He felt as though he were walking through quicksand.

He turned and tried to stumble back, becoming more alarmed as his steps became slower and his energy dwindled. He shouted for help. The few people winkling besides his father were too far away to hear him, however, and no one else was swimming.

Gary soon became weak and tired from his exertions, but the desperate will to survive drove him on. He urged himself forward, quietly whimpering with fear and pain, each movement of his body tearing at his aching muscles.

A few minutes ago he had not taken the situation seriously. It did not seem possible that he could be harmed, let alone killed, by barnacles. Now, though, he saw how easy it would be for him to topple forward, face first, and drown in a couple of feet of seawater, unable to raise himself above the gentle tide.

Gary's determination was formidable. He would *not* let himself be defeated by a lot of stupid barnacles. If it took all night he would somehow manage to get back to dry land.

And so he did—almost.

Gary had dragged himself to a point where the water was only nine inches deep, when he glanced down and saw that the barnacles now covered his body up to his navel. He had been so absorbed in getting back he had not noticed them creeping up.

Gary lost his balance then, and plunged, gasping, into the water. He was more weighted down than ever now, as the barnacles which had climbed from his legs to his waist had been replaced by others. He thrashed about wildly. For a few seconds he managed to keep his face above the water. But before he could shout for help, his mouth was full of salty barnacles and tentacles of slimy seaweed. His father might have heard him from that distance. He might have seen him, too. But he would not be able to now, because Gary's prone body was completely covered in seaweed and barnacles.

In his last few seconds of consciousness Gary saw nothing. He had opened his eyes underwater and barnacles had slid over the exposed eyeballs. The barnacles soon crammed themselves into his nostrils, his ears, and all over his head, back and arms, until he stopped moving.

Soon, Gary's father decided it was time to go home. He shouted for Gary several times, but there was no sign of the boy.

"Silly devil," he muttered to himself, surveying the empty horizon.

Sighing, the man began to search for more winkles while he waited for his son to return. But there were not many winkles left now; just lots and lots of barnacles.

DEAD LETTER

ALAN W. LEAR

WHEN you think about it, Fear's got all sorts of different ways of coming into people's lives. Sometimes it's sneaky about it, climbing at dead of night through the back window you forgot to fasten. Sometimes it's bold and knocks on your front door. Sometimes it lies in wait for you in the busy High Street, or in your doctor's surgery when you go for the results of your last check-up.

And sometimes it simply drops in through your letterbox.

An envelope's safe while it's sealed, like a hand grenade with the pin in place. Think a moment before you rip it open. Are you sure you'll find nothing but the latest news from your Auntie Moira in Stoke Newington? Are you sure Fear isn't lurking inside, waiting to be unleashed like some gruesome genie out of a bottle?

Fear came to our house on Friday morning, just over a week ago. "Bills, bills, bills!" Dad moaned, slitting his mail with the knife he'd used to butter the toast. "And still more blooming bills! It's all I ever see!"

"Watch your time for work, dear," Mum remarked to her fried eggs.

"I am. Strewth—five letters, and bad news in every one of them. Anyone would think we were back in old Tom Gannock's time."

"Tom who?" I asked.

"If you let your breakfast get cold, Robin, you'll eat it anyway." That was Mum.

"I was just asking—"

"I know you were. And I was just saying—"

"Tom Gannock," Dad answered me. "He used to be the village postman, son. Years ago, long before you were ever thought of."

People who live in cities take their mail delivery for granted. I've a bunch of cousins in Birmingham who couldn't tell you their postman's name if their lives depended on it. Things are different in the country. A little village like Upper Hallows, buried deep in darkest Somerset, looks on the man who brings the letters as a vital link with the outside world.

For the past few years, Larry Green's been the postie in these parts. Up before dawn he is every morning on his little moped, delivering to the village and the farms and the campsites for miles around. Always perfectly punctual, whatever the weather. Mum says she doesn't need an alarm clock, not when she's got the putt-putt of Larry's moped to wake her at five to seven.

"1950 I think it was," Dad murmured, rising from the table. "No, '51. A really bad year for the village, too."

"What was, love?" asked Mum.

"The year Tom Gannock was postman. Just one calamity after another, it was. Started with that outbreak of foot-and-mouth, and ended with me marrying you."

"Charmed," said Mum. I wolfed down the last of my bacon and eggs and picked up my schoolbag. Dad reminisced on.

"Seriously, though. Don't you remember how every post for months seemed to bring news of disaster? Mrs Price's son was killed in Korea, the bank foreclosed on George Carling's farm, poor Miss Austin got word that her hospital tests were positive . . . It got to be a village proverb: 'Tom Gannock never brings good news.' And, of course, the year wasn't half over when he—"

"Tom Gannock?" A voice like a bull's bellow rattled the

china on the Welsh dresser. "What the blazes has Tom Gannock to do with anything?"

Into the kitchen plunged my Uncle Frank, looking as if he wanted to fight the tables and chairs. He was a squat, broad man with fiery red hair, and a way of seeming to fill up small rooms so that the other people in them pressed up close to the walls. He was my dad's elder brother.

"Nothing, Frank, nothing at all." Dad almost cringed, although he was in his own house. "How's your head this morning?"

"My head? What's the matter with my head?"

To which the proper reply would have been, "Nothing, it'd make a lovely football." But no one would have the nerve to talk to Uncle Frank like that. I'd never seen a head as spherical as his. His nose had wide nostrils that bristled with stiff red hairs. His eyes were close-set, red-rimmed and full of suspicion.

"I only meant that you downed a good few pints last night," Dad muttered.

"Bacon and eggs, Frank?" asked Mum. "There's some letters for you on the sideboard."

"Just coffee." Uncle Frank turned his head to glare at Mum, as if he was challenging her to say he *couldn't* have just coffee. She returned his stare coolly from the Aga. Suddenly it seemed to me that they were going to stand like that for the rest of the day, for the rest of the winter —the little woman in her calico apron and the huge, dangerous man in the yellow-and-red checked suit with the wide lapels, both of them ready to drop dead sooner than look away first.

"Remember to save the foreign stamp for Robin," Dad said, breaking the spell.

Uncle Frank picked up his handful of bills and circulars and started to shuffle through them.

"What kind of stamp?" I asked. "Is it Canadian? Let's have a look."

There were six envelopes, and they were all buff-coloured but one. It was white—or it had been once, until someone left it overnight on a compost heap. You could hardly make out the address for the brown and green stains all over it, especially since the handwriting looked like a spider crawling across the paper. Thinking back, I remember the feeling of disgust that seized me when I looked at that envelope, as if the last rasher of bacon had been off. I glanced at the stamp.

"That's not foreign! It's British, a George VI penny red. That's no good to me."

"George VI?" Dad moved closer to look over Uncle Frank's shoulder. Mum did the same.

"Who'd stick a stamp that old on a letter?" she asked.

"It's not even in decimal money."

"I'm surprised Larry Green delivered it."

"Maybe someone found it and didn't notice—"

"Stone the crows!" Uncle Frank roared. "Can a man have some room to read his flaming letter!"

We all retreated sharpish as he gored the envelope with his thumbnail. Dad gave me a nod to get a move on if I wanted a lift to school. In the kitchen doorway, I paused and glanced back at Uncle Frank. He'd pulled out a sheet of writing paper and was squinting at it with his little eyes. I could see it was in just as grotty condition as the envelope—earth stains and patches of mould mottled the back.

Uncle Frank's eyes blazed.

"What's this?" he demanded. Windows and doors shook. "Someone thinks he's funny, eh? Someone having a joke with me? Is that it? Eh?"

Dad grabbed my shoulder and bundled me out to the car. I wasn't a bit sorry to leave.

When I was younger, it seemed incredibly romantic that my father's family had a black sheep in it. I was always hearing references to "that rascal Frank" at weddings and funerals, and from time to time Dad would get a letter from Canada that turned him moody for days. Those Canadian stamps were the start of my collection.

I knew Uncle Frank had eloped with the vicar's daughter and emigrated before I was born—she would have been my Auntie Clara, but she died of 'flu in Vancouver. I used to imagine Frank as a brave, flashing-eyed adventurer out of the comics. A pirate, maybe, or at the very least a gold prospector who'd return to Upper Hallows one day with sacks full of money.

The truth turned out a bit different.

One day, Larry Green brought an airmail letter that put Dad in a complete tizzy. Next thing I knew, I was moved out of my bedroom and into the attic, and Uncle Frank was upon us.

He wasn't debonair, dashing and loaded with doubloons. He was broke, ill-tempered and totally without a sense of humour. I'd hoped he'd tell me stories about life in Canada, but he hardly seemed to notice I existed. He spent every evening at the Goose and Feathers, and every day at race meetings up and down the country. To judge by the permanent grim set of his jaw muscles, he didn't have any spectacular success at them.

In less then a week, I'd decided I was heartily sick of my Uncle Frank. Then the George VI letter arrived.

Mum and I were watching telly that night when Dad came in from the pub. That was odd: he usually stays till closing time on darts nights.

"Anything the matter, honey?" Mum asked as he started laying newspaper on the carpet and fetching brushes and tins of polish. He always cleans his shoes when his nerves need calming.

"That brother of mine."

"Knocking it back, is he?"

"As if it was going out of fashion. But that's not all. He's got himself barred from the Goose and Feathers now. He picked a fight with young Charlie Perkins—said he kept staring at him. The saloon bar was half wrecked."

"Charlie Perkins can't fight. He's got a withered arm."

"That didn't stop Frank. When they chucked him out of the Goose he set out up the road to the Mount Royal Hotel. Heavens knows what state he'll be in when he gets home."

Mum shook her head. "We shouldn't have to put up with this, you know," she said very quietly.

"He's my brother." Dad polished furiously at his brown brogues; you could tell he was feeling utterly miserable.

Said Mum, "I knew there was something wrong with him when he got back from Newmarket. I could hear him for over an hour, pacing up and down the bedroom and muttering to himself. And at the dinner table, he kept taking that letter out of his pocket and reading it, over and over. You know, the one that came this morning."

"That reminds me." Dad put down his shoe brush and looked straight at me. He'd a spot of brown polish on the tip of his nose; I'd have laughed, but his expression was serious.

"That reminds me. Larry Green was in the Goose this evening. I mentioned to him how odd it was, someone sticking an out-of-date stamp on that letter. D'you know what he said? He said he'd never delivered it. If there'd been a letter like that in his sack, he'd have been knocking on our door to collect the excess postage."

"But I found the letter myself," said Mum. "It was on

the mat with the rest of the post when I got up this morning."

"That's right," Dad agreed. He was still looking straight at me. "So either Larry Green's a liar, which he's not, or the letter found its way on to the mat some time last night. Isn't that so, Robin?"

The next hour or so was taken up with one of those pointless, horrible conversations everyone goes through from time to time—you know, the sort that starts with, "Have you got anything you want to tell us?" and ends with lost tempers and dire threats. I swore an oath on the entire Bristol Rovers Football Club that I'd never had a George VI penny red in my stamp album, and that in any case I wouldn't spoil my collection for the sake of a stupid joke. I think Mum believed me, and maybe Dad did too; but by the time I went up the attic stairs to bed, I felt as if I were the chief suspect in the dock at the Old Bailey.

Maybe you can put the nightmare I had that night down to the rotten frame of mind I was in. Maybe. All I know is, it's the only one I'd had for four years, since my cousins in Birmingham showed me my first and last video nasty. And that I never want to be that scared again, ever.

It started pleasantly enough. I opened my eyes and found I was lying in my own warm bed in my own familiar bedroom. I felt fine. I felt like a million dollars. I knew that school was two whole days away. In the darkness I could make out my wardrobe, my dartboard on the door, my model aeroplanes in a line on the mantelpiece. I hadn't a care in the world. It was grand to be alive.

Then Fear came sneaking in.

I realised I shouldn't be in my own bed at all. Why wasn't I in the attic? Hadn't my bedroom been given to . . . given to . . .

I couldn't put a name to the person who'd got my bedroom. I couldn't put a face to him either. All I knew was, the fact that he existed was suddenly enough to fill me with unimaginable horror.

Something was wrong, badly wrong. I was in danger. Above all, I was in danger if I got out of bed. That was the one thing I mustn't do, the worst thing in the world, the thing that would mean the end of me for sure.

I got out of bed.

As I crossed the carpet to the window, I noticed I was wearing my football strip and that one of the bootlaces was undone. I took hold of the curtains and pulled them open.

Tons of earth were pressing against the window pane. The house had been buried while I was asleep. I stood there in the darkness, staring wide-eyed at the packed brown soil outside, moist and granular and squirming with worms.

Only I wasn't staring at it. I was part of it. Someone had buried me—me, not the house. The earth was pressing wetly against my chest and my fingers and my eyelids and my lips.

I opened my mouth to scream, and the earth fell in and filled it. I could taste it on my tongue, gritty and sour.

I tried to swim up through it, to claw my way to the surface. But the weight of the earth forced me down. Worms, damp and slimy and purple, wrapped around my hands and throat to hold me captive. And not just worms. Sharp, hard fingers of bone seized my ankles and pulled me still deeper, deeper into the crawling darkness.

Then I found I could speak after all, in spite of the dirt in my mouth. "You've got to let me go!" I repeated over and over. "I'm a special delivery."

And a voice like fingernails down a blackboard

41

answered, "No, you're not. You've come back marked 'Not known at this address'. You're a dead letter, my lad, and that's how you've got to stay for the next thirty years."

Saturday morning was grey and discouraging. After breakfast I stood on our doorstep and thought about going back to bed. The sky was the colour of dirty wool, almost low enough to reach up and touch. At the foot of the hill leading to the village, Croome's Acre was a disgusting quagmire. The birds in the hedgerows were trying to sing, but you could tell their hearts weren't in it. Even the tails of the wagtails weren't wagging that Saturday morning.

As I trudged down to Mrs Benson's general store, something white caught my eye in the grass of the roadside ditch: the only bright object in a drab, depressing landscape. I picked it up. The sight of spidery handwriting made my heart lurch.

It was the letter from the envelope with the George VI stamp. Uncle Frank must have crumpled it up and thrown it in the ditch on his way to the pub last night.

Carefully—because it was damp and disintegrating from its night in the open—I uncrumpled it. Touching it gave me goose pimples. It was like touching toadstools, or cold dead flesh.

The damp had obliterated some of the writing, but I could make out enough to feel very puzzled indeed. What was there in *this* to make Uncle Frank so upset?

Thursday

Dear Frank,
   I hear you've come home after all these years to look up your old pals.
   Hope we'll be able to have a get-together very soon.

—wishes, I suppose. The signature was just a foul black blur.

"Oh oh, here comes trouble!" said Mrs Benson, laughing, as the bell on the shop door went ping.

My rotten mood lifted at the sight of her. Anybody's would. You couldn't be depressed when Mrs Benson was around, bustling in her white overall and chuckling all over her plump pink face.

I was after sweets. In the part of the shop between the stationery and the garden furniture stood tier after tier of big glass bottles—each as tall as a toddler—full of cinammon balls, sugar bonbons, jelly babies and Mrs Benson's unique home-made acid drops.

"What do you mean, trouble?" I demanded, pretending to be indignant.

"Oh, my heart always sinks when I see you coming down the hill. I always says to myself, 'Here's that Robin Fogarty—sure sign of coming disaster, he is?'"

"You make me sound like Tom Gannock," I said with a laugh.

For a moment, it seemed as if a cold wet wind blew through the shop; but I'd shut the door behind me.

Mrs Benson's bushy eyebrows rose. "Fancy you coming out with that! I haven't heard Tom Gannock's name these thirty years."

"Quarter of acid drops, please," I said, suddenly anxious that she wouldn't say any more on the subject.

But her eyes were already misty with memory. "Tom Gannock . . ." she murmured as she weighed out the sweets. "He was a peculiar soul and no mistake. Never knew a chap who kept himself so much to himself. Hardly ever spoke a word, unless it was 'Registered letter: sign here please'. Lived all alone in a caravan on Croome's Acre, with never a friend in the world." Her face took on a look of deep sadness—it was scary to see Mrs Benson sad, and I wished she'd talk about something else. "Leastways, no friend but Clara Small, the vicar's daughter."

"My Auntie Clara?"

"That's right. Folk said she married Frank Fogarty in despair. He'd never have had a chance of winning her if Tom Gannock had stayed in the village."

"He'd have been my uncle, then," I said.

"Don't be daft. Frank's your Dad's brother, nothing can change that. Poor Clara'd have been no relation of yours if she'd married Tom. Maybe she'd be alive today if she had . . . and happy too, for all Tom was such a sinister customer."

There was something wrong with the shop. It was bigger than it should have been—the ceiling was dangerously high, and the walls leaned at precarious angles. The light seemed to be flickering. The tall shelves, laden with boxes of cornflakes and ball bearings, tins of lighter fuel and beans, bottles of bleach and American Cream Soda, began to tilt and topple toward me. Any minute now they were going to fall down and I'd be crushed, trapped . . . buried . . . I wanted to run out into the open air and safety, but I didn't. Instead I asked, "How do you mean, sinister?"

Mrs Benson shrugged. "Skinny chap, not a lot of flesh on his bones. He'd stooped shoulders and long, awkward fingers. He looked—what am I trying to say?—a bit Hallowe'en-like. Children used to cower under the bedclothes when they heard the creaking of his old rusty bike in the dark before dawn. No modern moped for Tom, of course . . . Here, Robin, are you all right?"

"Sure," I said. And suddenly I was. My moment of dread was over. The shop was its proper size again.

"It seems crazy when I look back on it now," Mrs Benson continued," but people really believed he was putting a curse on the letters he delivered. They started muttering, crossing the street to avoid him. Poor Tom! I can just imagine him, day after day, all alone in his caravan, knowing folk were hating him for the bad news he kept on bringing.

"In the end, he just up and left the village. Not a word to anyone, not even Clara. Just disappeared like snow off a dry-stone dyke. Next thing we knew, your Uncle Frank had married Clara and they'd run off to Canada together. And two years after that . . ."

Mrs Benson heaved a great sigh. The bright colours faded from the jelly babies in their jar.

"Sad old world, isn't it?"

A right blooming load of laughs that weekend was, I can tell you. Just to put the tin lid on it, Bristol Rovers lost at home. Uncle Frank spent all day Sunday hunched up in the living-room armchair like a red-faced thundercloud, snarling at the canary until it was scared to open its beak.

The only good thing was that I didn't have any nightmares on Saturday or Sunday night. When Monday morning arrived, I dressed and hurried down for breakfast.

There was another horrible soiled envelope lying on the sideboard, with another thirty-odd-year-old stamp stuck in the corner.

That night, Uncle Frank got himself barred from the Mount Royal Hotel. Dad locked up my stamp album and polished every shoe in the house.

Now some folk are early risers, and some folk are late

risers. I've a cousin in Penzance who'd snore till kingdom come if his mother didn't drag him bodily out of bed.

But with me, it's as if I've got an alarm clock implanted between my ears. That Monday night, I made up my mind I was going to be up and about with the dawn on Tuesday, in plenty of time to catch the joker who was queering my pitch with his stupid letters.

At five on the dot my eyes opened. By ten past I was out of bed, dressed and shivering at the attic window.

Not that I could see anything out of it. The sun wasn't anywhere near ready to rise yet. The sky hadn't a moon or a star to let you know it was there. The window pane might have been coated in tar. For half an hour or so I sat staring into the drooping eyes of my own sleepy, gormless-looking reflection.

Somewhere out there was the road. Somewhere out there was my dad's battered old Austin. Somewhere out there was the oak tree I fell out of on my ninth birthday, and that useless square of land called Croome's Acre where not even nettles would grow. And somewhere out there was the man with the mouldy, ancient, earth-smelling letters. I could almost feel him drawing closer as I sat and watched.

And then, at about a quarter to six, I could *hear* him drawing closer. I'd expected footsteps, but he didn't come on foot. Instead, out of the utter darkness, I heard the agonised creak . . . creak . . . creak . . . of an old rusty push-bike being laboriously pedalled up the steep slope.

I've never turned so cold so quickly. Suddenly I felt as I had in Mrs Benson's shop—as if the room and the house around me had expanded to twice their normal size.

Only I knew that nothing had got bigger. It was me—I'd got smaller. I was a tiny, helpless, squirming worm that a man could crush underfoot without even noticing. And coming up the hill, coming straight for me, was the biggest, most terrible thing in the world.

I could hardly breathe. I was back in my nightmare. Cold earth was packed tightly round me, its chill dampness seeping into my bones.

Creak . . . creak . . . creak . . . Silence. The bike had stopped outside. In the long, long minutes that followed, the beating of my heart seemed loud enough to wake the village. Then came the clack of the letterbox and the flop of a single letter landing on the mat.

The spell broke. I could move again, and I did. After all, it wasn't necessary for me to go out and confront the man on the road. I could just peep around the door, see who he was and tell Dad. In an instant I was out of the attic and dashing down the stairs.

There was someone else ahead of me.

The front door slammed open. I caught no more than a second's glimpse of a massive shape in red and yellow checks, plunging out into the night. He didn't even stop to pick up the letter.

I ran out in his wake. If there was going to be a fight, I wanted to be at the ringside. Uncle Frank would make mincemeat of the joker—and serve him right for turning me into a suspect.

The chill of the night air cut through me. I looked around, listening for the sound of battle, but the hill was silent. Not even the rustle of a mole digging. The night seemed to have swallowed Uncle Frank in a single gulp.

Reluctantly, I began to walk down the hill. My eyes made out a little bright patch of something on the far rim of the wayside ditch. When I picked it up I saw it was a picture postcard, showing a lump of modern sculpture and an inscription that read, "Festival of Britain, 1951."

I crossed the ditch. A steep slope of grass and mud

47

descended to Croome's Acre. I could see a scrap of white a few yards down; and another beyond it, and another beyond that.

Letters: strewn in a long straggly line on the ground like a game of Hare and Hounds.

I followed the trail down the slope. It was hopelessly slippery underfoot—I skidded and tripped and stumbled and was covered with mud before I got half way. Then I collided with a huge clump of gorse, blacker than the blackness of the night, that tore my clothes and skin as I desperately battled to force my way through it.

And I *had* to get through it. Why? Because I could see Croome's Acre through the branches, and what was happening down there.

The muddy ground was littered ankle-deep in postcards, parcels and letters, and in the midst of them Uncle Frank was struggling for his life. His attacker was tall and skinny and stooped, and he had Frank's throat gripped in two bone-white, clutching hands. I couldn't see his face. He was dressed in black serge and wearing a peaked cap.

Neither of the men made a sound as they fought there in the mud.

For all Uncle Frank's strength, he couldn't shake loose from the thin man's grip. His little eyes were bulging, his tongue was half out of his mouth and his cheeks were a dark, ugly purple. He was kicking and punching and heaving at his attacker, but as I beat at the barbed stems of gorse I could see that his legs were giving beneath him and his struggles growing weaker.

Now, folk tell you you should think before you act, plan ahead, count ten before you do anything rash. I didn't. It didn't occur to me that Uncle Frank probably deserved everything he was getting. It didn't occur to me that this

48

was my chance to get my bedroom back. It didn't even occur to me to be terrified.

I crashed out of the gorse bush at last, half-fell down the slope and across the muddy ground of Croome's Acre, and leaped with a yell on to the thin man's back.

It was like grabbing a sack full of waste paper. His body crackled where I gripped it. I wrapped my legs around his waist and my arms around his chest. Taken by surprise—it must have been the surprise that did it, not my pretty feeble strength—he let go of Uncle Frank's throat and reared backwards, spinning round to try and dislodge me.

I was almost choked by the smell of mould and dust and decay.

Uncle Frank fell into the paper-strewn mud, half unconscious. I clung on to the stranger's back for grim death—and if you know of a better way to describe what I was doing, go ahead and write your own story.

He reached back with bony hands, but he couldn't get hold of me. He twisted his head but he couldn't see me—under the celluloid rim of his cap, I just caught sight of empty eye-sockets in a yellow-white, fleshless face.

He kept turning round and round and round, faster and faster. My head spun. My hands, locked together in front of him, began to sweat and slip apart.

Then Uncle Frank came to enough to see what was happening. He staggered to his feet, raised fists and swung at his attacker's chest. There was a sound like jumping in a pile of dead leaves. With the first blow, I felt the thin man double up. With the second . . .

No point in not saying it. With the second, I was lying in the mud and holding on to nothing. Underneath me was a shapeless rag of black serge cloth, and near my head lay the rotted-through remains of a peaked cap. And besides that, nothing but crumpled paper. Dozens of hard, stiff

I caught sight of empty eye-sockets . . .

balls of it, all typewritten or scribbled on in pencil, black ink, blue ink and crayon. One of them, lying at my bewildered uncle's feet, was big and grim and vaguely in the shape of a human skull.

Next moment, a wind like the end of the world was sweeping across Croome's Acre. It caught Uncle Frank and knocked him into the mud. It howled like a Fury deprived of its dinner. And it picked up every ball and square of paper, every letter and postcard and parcel and bill, and the black serge jacket and the celluloid cap, and swirled them together up into the sky, for mile after mile, until no matter how I strained my eyes I couldn't see them any more.

I got up off the ground eventually. Uncle Frank was sitting in the mud with his head buried in his hands. His red and yellow checked suit was plastered with filth. He was mumbling—not to me, I don't think he realised I was there—in a voice like a small boy who's been caught red-handed.

"I didn't mean to do it. I only wanted to talk to him, to scare him a bit. I only wanted him to know that Clara was my girl and he should leave her alone. But he just sat there and never said a word, and I got angry and gave him a shove . . . that's all it was, just a shove . . . and he fell and struck his head . . . It was an accident. He must *know* it was an accident . . ."

I hung about, feeling embarrassed. The sky was getting quite light now. I heard a blackbird singing at the top of the hill. At length, Uncle Frank stood up, saw me, and suddenly had a brown leather wallet in his hand.

"Here—you—four fivers. It's all you're getting, so don't bother asking for more. You're to promise never to tell a soul what happened tonight. You got that? I don't want them coming round here with spades and digging down until they find . . . Have you got that? Not a soul!"

51

I promised. For four fivers, I'd have promised to become a Bristol City supporter.

So why am I breaking my promise now? Why am I writing the story down, so you can read it? I'll tell you.

Uncle Frank left Upper Hallows that same day, and a week's gone past since then. This morning I woke up with a start at quarter to six, and I heard the creaking of a rusty old bike coming up the hill outside. Then the sound of something being pushed through the letterbox.

It's here on the table in front of me as I write. King George VI is on the stamp. He doesn't look happy.

I haven't opened the letter yet, but I'm going to soon. No one else has the right, because the envelope has my name on it.

I don't know what's inside, but one thing I do know. It won't be good news, that's for sure.

HOUSE OF HORROR

Sydney J. Bounds

I won't be frightened, Mark Johnson told himself fiercely.

Even in the daytime, he imagined, little light would reach the cellar through the single small window set high in the wall and grimed with years of dirt. By night, the shadows beyond the ring of candlelight shifted and made strange shapes. Why should the candle flicker when there was no draught? And exactly what were they shadows of?

There were only three others present—Toby, Hog and Sue—and the shadows didn't match up.

"This is an old house with a long history of haunting . . ."

Toby's drone didn't carry the doom-laden tone he intended; his voice was too preachy to build up an eerie atmosphere. It was obvious that he didn't believe in ghosts, no matter how hard he pretended.

The smell in the cellar made Mark's stomach queasy; a smell derived from yellowing newspapers and cardboard cartons, oily rags and plastic bags that had contained rotting fruit or vegetables, milk bottles that had never been washed. That's what the cellar really was, he thought: a rubbish dump.

"Nobody knows how it started," Toby said. "There's a story that the house was cursed by one of the builders, who accidentally cut his finger with a trowel. Dripping blood on the foundations, he damned the house to Hell."

Mark, just turned thirteen, was the new kid in Northend—and if he passed this initiation test, he'd be accepted as one of the gang. It had been Toby's idea to meet in the cellar of the local haunted house—by candlelight, no torches allowed.

"The original owners of the house—" Toby squinted through rimless spectacles, scanning the small print of a discoloured newspaper—"were a young couple whose stay here ended in tragedy. Their baby died soon after birth, and rumours started to the effect that the Devil had claimed it. They moved away shortly afterwards."

Something fell with a squishy *plop* in the shadows, and Sue gave a little squeal. Toby had challenged Mark in front of Sue, a pert redhead in jeans, so, of course, he couldn't back out.

"The next owner didn't last long either." Toby's voice positively gloated; he was enjoying this recital, Mark realised.

Toby Bullivant was two years older than the others, tall and gangling. He dominated the gang with his voice, cold and honed like a blade, a voice that implied he knew it all. "This one was killed when he fell through a window, and a piece of glass cut his throat."

"Cut his throat," Hog echoed, fascinated. Hog was big for his age, broad and solid, a born follower in a black leather jacket. His habit of echoing Toby's words began to irritate Mark.

"Now the house wasn't so easy to sell. Over the years it stood empty for long periods and, when someone did take it, they left in a hurry. There were rumours that strange things happened in the house."

Well, Mark thought, it was certain that no one had lived here for a long time, whatever the reason. Getting through the front garden, with weeds up to his thighs, had

54

been like hacking a path through a jungle. No wonder local children crossed to the opposite side of the street when passing.

"The last person to buy the place is still alive," Toby said, and paused. "In a mental hospital. He was a stage magician—*but who knows what he conjured up*?"

Mark had an uneasy feeling that something lurked just beyond the wavering ring of candlelight. Once before, on holiday in the West Country, he'd visited a house that made him nervous—and discovered afterwards that it was supposed to be haunted.

He heard a scuttling sound. Rats in the walls? Or something else? Had Toby rigged up some nasty surprises? Should he warn the others?

Sue screamed, "A spider!"

It plopped down near her, huge and black and hairy, and a sudden draught blew out the candle. In the darkness, she panicked and led a mad rush for the door.

Mark was the last to move. He bounced off Hog and staggered back. The door slammed.

"Toby?" he called. "Sue? Hog?"

His only answer was the echo of running footsteps on the stairs beyond the cellar. The darkness was pitch black. Where were the matches Toby had brought to light the candle? He found them on the floor, struck one and looked around; he was alone. He tugged at the door but it wouldn't open.

Keep calm, he told himself. It's part of the test: scare me first, then lock me in the dark.

The match went out, and he waited for what seemed several minutes to see if Toby was going to spring any more shocks. Then he relit the short stub of candle and inspected the cellar. He found only discoloured walls and a litter of rubbish; there was one door and a small window too high to reach.

Unoiled hinges squealed, and the door swung slowly open.

"Toby?"

He waited, but there was no answer. Mark's scalp tingled. He crossed to the doorway and lifted the candle high, lighting the cellar steps. They were empty, and nobody could have had time to reach the top.

Mark went through the doorway and started up the steps, shielding the small, flickering flame with one hand. The walls seemed to close in about him. Imagination, he decided uneasily; it could only be an effect of shadows moving.

But he was glad when he reached the top of the stairs. The ground floor stretched away before him, bare boards and relics of furniture and dust everywhere. A full moon shone in through dingy windows, and he blew out his candle; he might need it before he got outside again.

In a slanting moonbeam, dust lifted as he moved, swirling into frightening grey shapes. Somewhere in the house a window slammed, and glass shattered with a sound like a gun-shot. He nearly jumped out of his skin.

He paused and took a deep breath before going on. In the silence, blood dripped. *Blood?* Of course it was only a tap dripping, monotonous, unnerving.

A pile of rubbish—mostly discarded paper—stirred as he approached, and skittered about the room, making small scuffling sounds.

Finally he reached the hallway and the bottom of the staircase leading to the upper floor; opposite was the front door and freedom. His ordeal was over . . .

Then, from upstairs, came the sound of sobbing, and he felt oppressed by an overwhelming sense of evil.

He called out: "Toby? Is that you up there?"

"Help me . . . please, help . . ."

Mark hesitated. It was Toby's voice, and it sounded as though he was in trouble.

Mark looked up into blackness and lit his candle again. Reluctantly he edged up the stairs, holding on to the banister rail. The treads seemed to move under his feet. It gave him a scary feeling and he reached the top more quickly than he intended.

A door slammed, cutting off the sobbing. He paused on the landing, looking along a passage. Part of the roof had caved in, and bright moonlight slanted through.

He saw a large wall mirror in a pealing gilt frame, the glass starred and coated with dust. As he moved, he watched his double ripple as if reflected in moving water. A second figure appeared in the mirror, a menacing shape stalking him from behind. He whirled about—and saw nothing more than a pile of rubbish moving in the breeze.

When his pulse slowed, he wondered: nothing? There was a suggestion of sly movement at the edge of his vision; something not quite seen but there all the same. And . . . was it his imagination, or had something touched his arm? A hand, moist and smelly . . .

A house couldn't have a life of its own—*could* it?

Then Toby began screaming behind a door further along the passage. Mark's breath became ragged and his heart pounded.

He knew that scream wasn't faked. Toby had been caught in his own trap. And Mark couldn't just leave him, even though the hairs on his neck bristled, and more than anything in the world he wanted to turn and run.

He forced himself to go on, his mouth dry with fear. He reached the door and rattled the handle; it was locked. From behind the wooden panels came panting sounds, like a dog with its tongue hanging out in a heat wave.

The door was old and rotting. Mark blew out the candle and dropped it on the floor, then took a step back and smashed his shoulder against the wood. The door burst inwards with violent force, coming off one hinge.

Toby Bullivant stood with his back against the far wall, his face grey as cheap paper and his spectacles two black discs where moonlight struck the glass. His voice came out as a whine.

"The house . . . it won't let me leave . . ."

His skinny body was unnaturally rigid, as if paralysed. He babbled nonsense as he stared at—*at what?*

Mark couldn't make out what it was at first; he knew only that he had to get Toby out of this house. Something stood between them, something grotesque and fluttery. Cloud passed the window, and the light of a full moon brightened the room.

Now Mark saw that the strange figure appeared to be composed of rubbish: scraps of cardboard and newspapers and plastic. The figure make by the house from odds and ends was terrifying; it towered above Toby, swaying like a cobra about to strike.

And Toby cowered before it.

Mark took an unsteady pace forward. The figure had eyes of milk bottle tops, glittering with malice; its teeth were broken glass and its claws were made from strips of a tin can. It was noseless.

It shuffled towards Toby on plastic-bag feet that dragged through the dust. Its purposeful advance was petrifying in the extreme. Mark felt as if every bit of heat was being sucked from his body.

Toby quivered like jelly, tears crawling down his cheeks, and his hands shook. He whimpered, "Help me, Mark . . . The others got away . . . The house wouldn't let me . . ."

Mark wanted to hold his nose. The ghastly figure smelt awful, reminding him that it was only rubbish, paper and rags and cardboard—and he fumbled for the matches in his pocket. With trembling fingers he brought out the box and dropped the first match, unlit.

Sweat froze like ice crystals on his forehead. He grasped three matches together and struck them. The heads flared into bright flame and he moved forward, holding them out till he touched the figure. Dry paper caught light and blazed up.

He dashed forward, seized Toby by one arm and dragged him towards the doorway.

"Run," he shrieked. "Run for it—now!"

Toby started shakily along the passage. Mark glanced back once at the burning figure as it twisted and writhed. Flames leapt high as it disintegrated, rags falling away and an oily smoke filling the room with a dark and pungent cloud.

Then he ran for the stairs, pushing Toby ahead of him. Their combined weight went through the rotting wood and the staircase collapsed. Toby fell and Mark jumped over him. At the bottom, he dragged Toby upright and out of the house.

"My leg," Toby gasped. Physical pain seemed to have overtaken his fear.

Mark put an arm under his shoulder to help him as he limped through the garden to the moonlit street beyond.

Presently they paused and looked back and saw an angry red glow at one of the high windows. Dense grey ash floated on the still night air. Mark Johnson shuddered as a long drawn out wail of despair faded away: the sound of a damned soul plummeting to Hell.

THE DIARY

Samantha Lee

THE SLEET WAS turning to snow over the North Sea as the train pulled into Inverness. It was as cold and uninviting as only a station can be at seven o'clock in the morning.

The man awaiting Mary on the platform was cold and uninviting too. The only spot of colour on his entire person was the whisky-veined nose that glowed raw red in the winter-dark morning. The rest of him, from the muddied leather of his boots to the indeterminate tweed of his cloth cap, was uniformly grey as the granite houses through which they were shortly to drive on their way out of town.

"Miss Mary, is it?" enquired the man, who went on, without waiting for an answer: "Aye, well I'm McNab. I've been sent to fetch you to Darktower."

The only other words he directed to her during the interminable five-hour drive were uttered about half way through their journey. He passed a flask and a parcel through from the front seat to where Mary sat huddled under plaid rugs in the back of the rattletrap Ford.

"You'll be hungry nae doubt," he said. "There's a meat piece and some skirlie for you in there."

Mary unwrapped the offering eagerly. Within the greaseproof shell she found a cold beef sandwich and a lump of what looked like congealed porridge. The tea at least was hot. Hot and sweet. She took a great gulp, burning her tongue, then attacked the food. It was surprisingly tasty. And she was ravenous. She'd had nothing to eat since beginning her long journey from London the night before.

As she chewed, she looked out at the seemingly endless succession of snowy crags towering over the mist-shrouded moorland and thought how different it all was from her native Hampstead with its cosy cafés and trendy shops.

A great surge of loneliness washed over her, and she had to bite her burnt tongue and remind herself that she was a big girl of eleven now, to stop herself from bursting into tears. She studied McNab's face in the rear view mirror. He didn't look like a man much given to sympathy.

Mary had never been to Scotland before. She was only here now because her mother and father had been killed in a car crash the month previously and had left her destitute and with only one living relative, her rich and eccentric Great Aunt Elspeth.

It was to Great Aunt Elspeth's that they were journeying.

Mary's very first visit to the Highlands.

And yet, as they wound their way through uninhabited country, where the occasional house stood out like a sore thumb, she couldn't help feeling that somehow, somewhere, she had done all this before. The feeling intensified when, in the early afternoon, she caught her first glimpse of their destination.

Darktower. Part house, part castle keep. It stood like a sooty finger against the snow-heavy sky. Sandwiched between a great overhang of rock and a fathomless mountain tarn, it looked about as welcoming as a mausoleum.

Mary shivered, hunching down into the tartans, wishing

61

herself a thousand miles away from that cheerless dwelling and her unknown great aunt.

"It's only for three weeks," she told herself, "then you'll be off to boarding school."

The thought did little to reassure her or to dispel the growing feeling that inside Darktower lay something as cold and menacing as its bleak façade.

The car drew up in front of massive oak doors, and McNab climbed stiffly from the cab, moving round to the boot to begin unloading the cases.

Above the curved lintel hung a weatherbeaten coat of arms. A wolf locked in mortal combat with a salamander. Great serrated teeth closed around the reptile's scaly neck. The giant lizard's open jaws screamed in silent supplication at the sky.

With a groaning of timber, the double doors swung inwards, and a small, plum figure scurried out.

Whatever Mary had expected, it certainly wasn't the smiling, red-headed girl who bustled over to the car and opened the door, helping her out with warm, reassuring hands.

"Miss Mary," she said. "Come in. You must be fair perished, the dreich day that it is. Come in to the warm. The Mistress is in the parlour waiting to see you."

Mary allowed herself to be led into the house, across a broad hallway paved with marble slabs and in through one of the many doorways that opened off it.

Entering the parlour was like stepping backwards in time. Maroon velvet curtains closed off any light that might have filtered in from the dark afternoon, and the air was unhealthily stuffy. Light from the roaring fire flickered on wood-panelled walls hung with stags' heads and round leather shields studded with iron. Above the fireplace, a giant claymore, double-edged fighting weapon of the clans, hung like the sword of Damocles over the hunched figure in the wheelchair.

"Close the door, Morag," scolded the figure. "There's a terrible draught."

Morag did as she was bid, then led Mary across to meet her last relative.

Great Aunt Elspeth looked at least a hundred years old. She was shrivelled and brown as an old leaf. Mary had to stoop to look into the wizened monkey face. Dulled eyes stared back at her. And stared. And stared. Something akin to recognition flickered behind the opaque pupils.

"Fiona?" The voice wavered on the question.

"No, Ma'am," said Morag gently. "This is Miss Mary, come all the way from London."

"Of course it is," said the old woman testily. "Do you take me for a fool?" The eyes assumed a hint of cunning. "Take her to Fiona's room. She'll be comfortable there."

Morag led Mary into the hall once more and up the wide, curved stairway to the gloom of the upper floor.

"I've lit a fire," she said chattily, "just to take the chill off the place."

The room was furnished in the same style as the parlour, but all the furniture was child-sized. A box bed had been built into the wall, and there was a miniature wardrobe and a dressing-table over which hung a delicately carved oval mirror. By the window, where it would catch the best of the light, stood a tiny writing desk complete with ancient stone inkwell and old-fashioned nibbed pen.

"It's lovely," said Mary, in genuine delight.

Morag shivered.

"It will be when it's warmed up a bit," she said. "It hasn't been used in years."

She bustled to the fireplace to throw another couple of

logs into the grate, and Mary followed her, holding her hands out to the rosy glow.

Above the mantel hung the portrait of a young girl in late Victorian dress.

"Who's that?" Mary wanted to know.

"That's Fiona," said Morag. "The Mistress's younger sister. She died young, poor quine." She trotted to the door. "And speaking of the Mistress, it's time for her nap. Why don't you take one too? You'll be fair tired after your journey. Tea's not for a couple of hours yet. I'll give you a call when it's ready."

For some time after she'd gone, Mary continued to scrutinise the portrait. There was something vaguely familiar about the features, the expression, the way the head was held slightly to one side.

She tried to place the resemblance but eventually gave up, moving to the dressing-table and slumping on to the petit point stool. She studied her face in the mirror. She *was* tired. Over her shoulder Fiona studied her too. It was then that it struck her. Except for the outmoded clothes and the elaborate, beribboned hairstyle, it might have been a portrait of herself.

She rose to take another look.

There was no doubt about it. The corn-coloured hair was darker than hers, the soft green eyes lighter, but apart from that she and Fiona might have been twins.

She studied the wistful face of the long-dead girl and was suddenly gripped again by the nameless panic she had felt on first approaching Darktower.

"I wonder how the poor thing died?" she thought to herself.

She was still wondering when, a few minutes later, she crawled into the box bed and fell into an exhausted sleep.

But she did not sleep well.

64

In her dreams, the dead Fiona descended from the confines of her frame to weep and cry at her side, wringing her rotting hands and wailing for help—but from what?

And then, Mary knew.

For into the room tottered the emaciated figure of Great Aunt Elspeth. She carried a feather pillow, and her narrow lips were drawn back in a hideous facsimile of a smile. She advanced on the box bed with a slow, deliberate tread.

Mary knew she was having a nightmare, knew too that it was imperative she wake up before the nightmare became reality. Nearer and nearer came Great Aunt Elspeth, an expression of utter evil cloaking her raddled features.

And then she was there. Beside the bed. Lowering the suffocating pillow towards Mary's face.

Mary made a supreme effort, opened her mouth and screamed herself awake.

Above her, the face of her great aunt floated like a blood-gorged moon. The expression of evil had been replaced by one of concern. A curled, arthritic hand reached out to stroke her forehead. Still in the grip of the dreadful dream, Mary cringed away.

"Tut tut," said the old woman. "Wake up, child. You've been having a bad dream. Tea's ready. Comb your hair and come down. We're waiting for you."

And then she was gone, with only the click of the closing door to prove she'd been there at all.

Mary lay rigid beneath the bedclothes until her pounding heart stilled and her limbs ceased their palsied shuddering.

Outside, the dark day had dimmed to an early dusk. She struggled from her bed and over to the wardrobe, to where McNab had left her suitcase and her overnight bag. Unzipping the small red holdall, she groped inside, feeling for her hairbrush. Her fingers closed around a piece of paper. She drew it out. It was yellowed and uneven down one side, as though it had been torn from some ancient notebook.

Mary held it towards the light of the glowing fire. Across its width, in perfect copperplate writing, was a cryptic message.

The left hand drawer of the escritoire.

What on earth could that mean?

Mary looked around the room. Her eyes lit on the writing desk. From her first year French she knew that *écrire* was the verb "to write". She crossed to the desk and pulled open the left hand drawer.

It was empty.

She eased the drawer right out of its groove and felt around the walls. The back seemed to be loose. She prised the false wall away. In the tiny, concealed recess behind it she found the diary.

It was bound in dark green leather, and on the front, tooled in gold, was a date.

1905.

On the flyleaf, in the same copperplate handwriting in which the note had been written, was the following inscription:

Fiona Fitzwalter . . . Aged 11 years.

Mary held the diary to the window to catch the last of the fading light. The dying sun streaked the clouds with carmine and bathed the book in a gory glow.

The diary was a chronicle of small horrors inflicted on one child by another. It started with verbal abuse and escalated through physical persecution to the strangling of a favourite kitten. In the unadorned prose of childhood,

Fiona had set down the chilling tale of how her deranged elder sister had made her short life a misery.

It had begun in the January when their beloved mother had died and their brother Jamie had been sent off to boarding school. Fiona had always been her father's favourite, and Elspeth became fanatically jealous. In effect, Mr. Fitzwalter, grieving for his lost wife, had little time for either of his daughters, and Fiona, not wishing to burden him with further worry, had carried the full weight of her sister's increasing irrationality on her own narrow shoulders.

The final entry made a cold chill of apprehension run down Mary's spine.

Things are becoming worse by the day, she read, *and I really do not know where I shall turn for help. It is selfish I know to think of my own problems when dear Papa is so poorly. But since his sudden illness Elspeth has become quite mad, saying that I have poisoned him. She swears that, should he die, she will kill me. If only Jamie were not at school. And there is no one else. In the presence of grown-ups Elspeth behaves like an angel, so who would believe me? Now Dr. Donald says that dear Papa may not last the night, and in truth, I fear for my very life.*

The rest of the pages were blank.

Mary glanced at the date of the last entry.

December 19th.

And *this* was December 19th. She knew because her railway ticket, bought the day before, had had December 18th stamped across it in large letters.

"What's this, then?"

The voice hissed, like a snake, in her ear. A liver-spotted hand darted over her shoulder to snatch the diary.

Mary turned to face her Great Aunt Elspeth. The face of the nightmare. Cunning. Evil. Insane.

67

The old woman flipped through the pages of the diary.

"Lies," she muttered. "All lies. It was her. She was the wicked one. Stealing Papa away from me. She deserved to die."

She peered at her grandniece suspiciously and narrowed her rheumy eyes. Mary stood rooted to the spot.

"You think you can fool me, Fiona?" she said craftily. "Calling yourself Mary. Crawling back here after all these years to make trouble. But you shan't. I was always smarter than you. I fooled them once and I can fool them again."

She hurled the diary into the fire. Flames licked around the dust-dry pages and it caught with a whoosh, shooting sparklers of light out into the darkened room.

Great Aunt Elspeth fixed Mary with her evil eye.

"You wait," she said. "Just you wait. I'll be back."

Then she limped from the room, locking the door behind her.

Mary dashed after her, banging and hammering, calling for help, pleading to be let out.

But if Morag or McNab heard her they gave no sign.

Outside the sun sank below the horizon, leaving her alone in the dark. Frantically she scrabbled for the light switch. But there wasn't one. The old house had never been wired for electricity.

Something inside Mary snapped. She screamed till her voice was hoarse, battered until her hands were bruised, but still no one came. At last, when what seemed like hours had passed, she crawled to the box bed and cried herself to sleep.

And the nightmare began again.

The same nightmare. The wailing Fiona climbing from her frame. The door opening to admit Great Aunt Elspeth. Her slow, inexorable advance on the bed.

Once more Mary screamed herself awake.

And again her great aunt's face hung over her.

But this time there was nothing solicitous about the expression. Demented eyes bored into her own, hypnotising her like a frightened rabbit.

And then she couldn't see the eyes any more, for something was over her face. A pillow. And she couldn't breathe.

She began to struggle, flailing with her arms and legs against the old lady's demoniacal strength, using up the last of her precious air in a final clawing attempt to keep a hold on life. The veins pulsed in her forehead. Her lungs felt on fire. She couldn't breathe. She was suffocating.

There was a deafening explosion in her eardrums, and fire flashed white behind her eyes.

And then . . . nothing.

Blackness . . . Emptiness . . .

The pressure eased on her face as the pillow was lifted. With sightless eyes she stared up at the old woman, saw the expression on her face turn from triumph to disbelief, from disbelief to terror.

Mary was dead. She knew she was dead just as she'd known she was dreaming before. And yet she still saw these things. It was as if she saw with someone else's eyes. Someone who had stepped inside her body and was reanimating the corpse.

She felt herself rise from the bed.

The old woman backed away from her, drooling like a baby.

Casually, Mary glanced back over her shoulder and was not surprised to see her body still prone on the bed. She felt light and triumphant. She caught sight of her reflection in the carved oval mirror and calmly noted that it was not Mary's reflection but Fiona's. And not the reflection of innocence depicted in the portrait. This was a gorgon head shrieking for revenge. Worm-eaten eyes blazed in a cadaverous face, the green-tinged flesh of which had stretched and split over the skull beneath.

She turned that fearful face towards the great aunt who was also her sister. And in her sister's face she saw only terror. Terror of the unknown, the unknowable and the final frightful knowledge that an old account was at last about to be settled.

Slowly she advanced across the room, holding skeletal claws out before her. Tattered flesh dripped like fetid icicles from the curved fingers, wafting up to her leprous nostrils the stench of her own decay.

Elspeth staggered backwards through the open door, towards the great curved stairway. Small, bleating sounds issued from the gaping mouth, and she shook uncontrollably as though in the grip of some dreadful ague.

Fiona-who-was-Mary smiled, exposing rotten teeth in decomposing gums.

"Now," she said, and the words gurgled like a death rattle. "Now it's *my* turn, Elspeth."

She reached forward, placed one tattered hand against her sister's shoulder. . . and pushed.

With a hoarse scream the old woman fell backwards, clutching desperately for the banisters, somersaulting on the worn carpet, bouncing off the panelled walls, her brittle bones shattering with each impact, until she came to rest, a disjointed puppet, on the chessboard floor of the hallway.

A hand was shaking her awake.

She opened her eyes.

Morag's freckled face, creased with worry, hovered so close that the buttermilk breath felt warm on her cheek.

Elspeth staggered backwards . . .

"Miss Mary," said Morag. "Come quick. Something dreadful's happened."

Mary sat up, rubbing the sleep from her eyes. Relief flooded over her. She swung her legs over the side of the box bed and stifled a yawn. Outside the window it was still light.

"How long have I been asleep?" she asked.

"Just since I left you, Miss," Morag answered. "About an hour."

She hurried out on to the landing.

Mary followed her.

"An hour . . .?" she said and then stopped, for Morag was pointing down into the hall.

An icy hand gripped Mary's heart. Gingerly she looked over the banisters.

Great Aunt Elspeth's body lay in a crumpled heap at the bottom of the stairs, just as it had done in the dream.

"I can't imagine how it happened," said Morag, and her voice sounded strange and far away. "She hasn't been out of the wheelchair in twenty years."

Mary swung round and rushed back into the bedroom, grabbing the left hand drawer of the writing desk and yanking it from its grooves.

When Morag entered a moment late she found Mary standing with the diary in her hand, staring at the inscription on the flyleaf.

Fiona Fitzwalter . . . Aged 11 years.

The older girl wrinkled her nose, moved to the window and flung it wide.

"It smells like something died in here," she said. "Oh, dear, I shouldn't be saying that, what with the mistress lying there. Oh well . . . I'd best go and find Mr. McNab. He'll have to fetch the doctor."

But Mary wasn't listening. She was leafing through the

72

pages, devouring snatches of the same dreadful tale that she had read in full during her nightmare.

It had been a nightmare . . . hadn't it?

She glanced up at the portrait. Fiona's expressionless face stared impassively back.

Mary lowered her head to re-read the final entry made on December 19th, 1905.

A tiny breeze from the window lifted the page and flipped it over.

Two words stood out on the paper with the clarity of blood against snow. Two words etched in the now familiar script. Two words that hadn't been there before and that told Mary all she needed—or didn't need—to know.

Two words.

Thank you.

SHADOW OF THE ROPE

ROGER MALISSON

"You are going to be the next big star of stage, screen and steam radio," announced Mike's Uncle Bill, closing the dressing-room door behind him. "According to your mother, that is. I just phoned to say we arrived safely, but I hardly got a word in. Next stop: Hollywood, she reckons."

Mike Wilkins grinned and put down his script of "In the Shadow of the Rope".

"Honestly, it's only a two days' telly job I've got, Uncle Bill! Hardly Oscar-nomination stuff. Mum gets so excited when I'm working, and Dad's worse, if anything—they make *me* nervous. I'm glad you're my 'minder' this time."

"So am I. I've never seen a television play being made," replied his uncle, settling into an armchair. "Now then, do you think you can remember your lines?"

"I'll try." Mike cleared his throat and called, "Penny for the guy, mister? Penny for the guy?"

"Briliant, lad. Perfectly memorised. How do you do it?" cried Uncle Bill in mock amazement, and they both burst out laughing. The character Mike was playing —Tommy Briggs, a murder victim—only had that one line. Still, it was Mike's first speaking part on TV and he was glad to get it. He'd never had to say anything on his own before, though he'd done quite a lot of work for the TV company since their casting staff had spotted him in a production given by his local amateur dramatic society a couple of years ago.

Mike loved acting, but he certainly wasn't starry-eyed about "the business". In spite of what his mum believed, he knew he'd only been given the part of Tommy Briggs because of his likeness to the slight, fair-haired kid who'd been bumped off by "Mad Jack" Hatchbury fifty years before. Each programme in the "Shadow of the Rope" series featured a famous trial intercut with reconstructions of the crimes. The series aimed to be realistic, and whenever possible it was filmed at the authentic locations. Because they showed photographs from the time, actors who resembled the original characters were always chosen for the main parts.

As if reading his thoughts, Bill picked up a copy of "In the Shadow of the Rope", the book which the television series was based upon, and opened it at the Jack Hatchbury case.

"You really are a dead ringer for Tommy Briggs, Mike," he said, studying the photographs. "I wonder if the actor playing Mad Jack looks as much like him? I'll bet it was a difficult match, though."

Mike agreed. Jack Hatchbury had an unusual face. At first glance it seemed friendly, even handsome, but looking closer you noticed that the mouth was thin and twisted under the black moustache, and that something was very odd about the half-closed eyes.

There was a light tap on the door and Chrissie appeared. She was a Production Assistant, a bright, chatty girl who had met them when they arrived at the studios.

"Ready, Mike? Good. We'll lock your cases in the dressing-room, Bill, till you come back. This way to Wardrobe!"

In the Wardrobe Department Mike was kitted out in a tattered shirt and short, baggy trousers, bulging socks and scruffy shoes, with a jacket and cap too small for him.

Then the make-up girls whisked him away. They grubbied his neck, hands and knees with dark cosmetics. Clever shading made his face seem thinner and his eyes larger. They trimmed his hair at the back and combed a gel through it to take off some of the shine. Within an hour Mike was transformed into the image of a half-starved, mucky little urchin; into the image of the long-dead Tommy Briggs.

Chrissie and Uncle Bill were waiting for him when he emerged from Make-up. Unnervingly, his uncle stared at him without recognition for several seconds, but Chrissie was delighted.

"Perfect, Mike! They've done a terrific job on you. You could be Tommy Briggs' twin!"

Bill looked quite shaken. "I didn't know you for a minute, lad," he said.

"Let's have some lunch," Chrissie suggested. "You must be hungry by now."

In the busy canteen nobody gave Mike a second glance. The three of them shared a table with a caveman, a Hell's Angel and a Jacobean lady, and Mike thought Chrissie and his uncle looked quite out of place in their modern clothes.

"Well, to business," Chrissie said towards the end of the meal. "You've read the script, haven't you, Mike? Then you'll know that Jack Hatchbury murdered several people in the 1930s, the last of whom was Tommy Briggs. He took Tommy to his house, promising him a penny for his guy, then stabbed him to death. Jack was caught, arrested and tried, and found guilty but insane. He escaped the rope, but he died in an institution a couple of years later."

"Was he always known as 'Mad Jack'?" asked Mike.

"Yes. At first it was an affectionate nickname, because Jack was rather eccentric and often played practical jokes.

76

But the name turned out to be horribly prophetic. No one who knew him suspected that there was a dark, sinister side to his nature—black moods when he'd destroy anyone who crossed his path."

"He had a split personality, then," said Uncle Bill.

"Exactly. Like quite a lot of murderers, Jack was good-looking and good-humoured, with a happy-go-lucky nature. But he could change . . . We'll be filming Tommy's murder tomorrow, at the spot where he was actually killed. This afternoon we're shooting the scene on the street corner where Tommy first meets Jack."

Mike glanced out of the window at the clear July day.

"But the script says it's a dark, snowy November evening," he pointed out.

"We'll be shooting 'day for night'," explained Chrissie. "The film will be under-exposed in the camera so that it will seem like dusk on the screen, and the sunshine will become moonlight."

Uncle Bill shook his head in amazement. "Nothing's ever quite what it seems, is it?"

"We can cheat most things," chuckled Chrissie. "Time to go now, if you're ready."

"What about the snow?" Mike asked as they followed her out to the car.

"You'll see."

He did indeed, when they arrived on location. A thick layer of coarse salt had been spread over the pavement and road. Slumped against a nineteen-thirties style gas streetlamp was a guy, stuffed with straw and dressed in rags. Seeing the set, Mike felt the beginnings of a familiar, restless excitement, half enjoyable and half fearful, which always preceded a performance.

Through the maze of people and equipment gathered for the filming, the series' director, a short, sandy-haired man named Clive, emerged to greet Mike while Chrissie quietly steered Bill to a spot where he could watch comfortably without getting in anybody's way. Clive put his arm round Mike's shoulder.

"Nice to see you again, Mike. You look exactly right," he said. "Come and meet our murderer, John Pocklington-Jones. "Jack!" he called, and a tall, slim, affable-looking man hurried over to join them.

"So this is my victim! Good to meet you, Mike. Do call me Jack, by the way—everyone else seems to have fallen into the habit, and it's close enough to John. My word, your casting department's done you proud, though, Clive! Young Mike is Tommy Briggs to the life—if that's the right expression!"

They laughed, and Clive said, "You might have seen Jack playing a cop in the 'Police Call' series, Mike —excuse me, I must have a quick word with Chrissie."

"Oh, of course! I remember now," said Mike. "Your make-up's so good that I didn't recognise you as the policeman. But there's something missing. . ."

"This!" cried Jack, producing something black and furry from his pocket. "No, it's not a dead rat, it's Mad Jack's moustache. It keeps falling off. Still, as long as the make-up ladies don't stick it on with superglue I don't mind . . . Oh, it looks as though they're nearly ready for us, Mike."

Jack went to have his moustache replaced and Clive began to rehearse Mike for the first shot.

"Remember, Mike, you're very cold. Looking for a passer-by . . . wondering if it's worthwhile staying any longer. Turn to your right, look up the street. Jack's shadow falls—you haven't heard him approach—you turn and look up, startled—then hopeful."

After a couple more rehearsals they were ready to begin filming.

"We're going for a take. Quiet please."

Clive nodded to the cameraman.

"Turn over."

"Camera's turning."

"Sound running."

"Mark it."

"Fifty-two, take one." The clapperboard slammed.

" . . . Action!"

Mike stamped his feet, shivering, surveying the street, blowing on his hands. A black shadow fell. He turned, catching his breath as he gazed up into the dark, morose face looming above him.

"Penny for the guy, mister? Penny for the guy?"

His voice surprised him. It sounded high and pleading, probably too scared.

"And . . . Cut! Very good, Mike. Thank you, Jack."

After two more takes Clive was satisfied. There was a pause while adjustments were made to the great film lights and the camera assistant changed the magazine on the camera, which was moved and angled to shoot Jack's face from Tommy's point of view. Mike had to say his "Penny for the guy" line out of shot while Jack, with a smile as false as the gas lamp that was supposed to be illuminating the scene, told him,

"All my money's at home. But I live just round the corner—come with me."

Then the camera moved back to film Jack setting off down the road with Tommy following him, trotting to keep up with his stiff-legged stride. There were other, briefer shots, and by the time Clive called the final "Cut!" Mike could almost believe that he really was the hungry orphan who had shivered at that same street corner fifty years ago, begging pennies from a sinister, smiling stranger. His hands felt cold and reality seemed far away.

"Tea-time!" sang Chrissie, breaking the spell. "Everybody back to Mad Jack's."

Bill appeared and walked beside him.

"Well, you didn't do too badly," he remarked, and Mike could have hugged him for his calm, reassuring presence and what was, from Uncle Bill, high praise.

"You weren't too bored, then?" he asked anxiously. "There's always such a lot of hanging about involved in filming."

"Not at all," replied his uncle. "It's fascinating stuff—I'm hooked!"

The house that had once belonged to Jack Hatchbury was a detached Victorian building with a drab, neglected air. Chrissie led them through the overgrown garden to the back door and into a large kitchen where tea, sandwiches and buns were waiting for them. Mike and Bill helped themselves and found a couple of chairs in a corner as the room filled with hungry, chatting technicians. The director joined them, beaming.

"Well, we fairly ripped through that sequence," he said. "In fact, we're slightly ahead of schedule. I was thinking that we might manage one more shot of Mike, now that we're in the house; that is, if we have enough time. . .?"

Because of his age, Mike was only allowed to perform for three hours in a day. He glanced appealingly at his uncle, who consulted his watch and agreed they had almost three-quarters of an hour.

"Great. It's a long shot of you lying in a pool of blood after you've been stabbed, Mike," Clive explained. "You know, of course, that we often shoot scenes out of sequence. Right, I'll go and set it up—don't rush your tea."

"He's very pleased with you," said Chrissie when Clive had gone. "I heard him telling the cameraman that he wished every actor had an attitude as professional as yours."

Mike glowed at the praise.

"By the way, where's Jack?" asked Uncle Bill, surveying the crowded room.

"Gone to the florists' to buy some flowers for his wife's birthday. I offered to go for him, but he said he wanted a walk— I don't think he likes being in this house very much. Goodness knows what the shop assistants will make of him in that awful overcoat and his Jack Hatchbury make-up—oh, talk of angels," she said, as Jack came through the door with an armful of roses.

"Got them!" he announced triumphantly. "There'd have been blue murder at our house if I'd forgotten her birthday. Dump these in water for me, would you, sweetie?" he added to one of the catering ladies. He gave her a handsome smile, and the flowers, and her cross look melted. She took the flowers to the sink and Jack poured himself a cup of tea.

"We're doing the shot of you standing over Tommy's dead body after this break," Chrissie told him.

"Oh, jolly good. Lots of gore, eh?"

"Tell me, how do you manage murders and such?" Bill asked. "Violence always looks so convincing on the screen."

"Well, Mike will be a couple of feet away from the knife, but the camera will be positioned so that they will seem close together when Jack attacks him. The rest is done with sound effects, recorded and dubbed on to the film afterwards."

"How do you do that?" asked Bill.

"Cabbages."

"I beg your pardon?"

Chrissie laughed: "Cabbages, I said! You see, if we

want the sound of a person being hammered, say, or decapitated or knifed, then we just bash, chop or slice into a cabbage. It makes a wonderful, authentic-sounding noise. Melons are good, too," she added thoughtfully. "Anyhow, in your case, Mike, we'll probably stab a cabbage."

"I want to know how Tommy was really murdered," said Mike. He hadn't been allowed to read "In the Shadow of the Rope" because the descriptions and photographs were too gruesome, and the script didn't give much detail.

"It seems that Jack felt genuinely sorry for the poor, and gave quite a lot to charity; he had a liberal, generous side to his nature," Jack began. "He saw Tommy on the street, obviously cold and hungry, and as far as we know he had every intention of giving him food and a few shillings. He took Tommy back to his house and made him wait in the front room. He found his wallet and went down to the kitchen for some bread. And then his eye fell on a long steel carving knife . . . I say, I'm not frightening you, am I?"

"Oh no," said Mike, "I've got a strong stomach, honestly. Haven't I, Uncle Bill?"

"Stronger than mine," said his uncle with a smile. "What happened then?"

"One of his black fits overcame him," said Jack in a mellow, thrilling voice.

"He seized the knife and hid it under his coat. Evil, muttering voices in his head were telling him to kill, for the boy was not fit to live and must be destroyed. He climbed the steps from the kitchen, hate in his heart, and went back to the room where Tommy was waiting.

"Instead of the promised money he drew the gleaming kitchen knife from his coat. He leapt at the terror-stricken

82

boy and stabbed him savagely through the neck. Tommy died almost instantly, blood spurting from his throat. Jack felt peaceful, almost happy; the voices in his head were silent at last, though blood spattered the very walls . . . He went into the kitchen and calmly cleaned his hands and the knife, and he burned his soaking overcoat. Then he switched on the radio to round off the evening with a bit of Beethoven, went to bed and slept soundly. His neighbours spotted him in the morning trying to dispose of the body; the alarm had been raised when Tommy was reported missing and his abandoned guy was found."

"You told that beautifully, Jack," said Chrissie, and the actor gave a little bow. "We were all enthralled—Bill looks a bit pale though!" She picked up her clipboard. "Come on, Mike, we'd better get you ready for the next shot."

She led the way up the half-dozen steps that led from the kitchen into the main part of the house, and into a small room, where a make-up artist began to daub "blood" from a bottle on to Mike's shirt and jacket.

"It looks very real," Bill remarked.

"Yes, it's good, isn't it? It comes in two colours, light and dark red, depending on which artery it's supposed to be oozing from—oh, please don't worry!" Chrissie added, seeing Bill's queasy expression. "It's just a harmless dye and it washes out in a jiffy—it's not like real blood at all."

"I think I'll just get a breath of air," said Bill, making for the door.

"My uncle's a bit squeamish, Chrissie," Mike explained.

"Good thing you're not," she said, ruffling his hair. "This way, Mike."

They walked along a narrow hall to the front room of the house where Tommy had been murdered. The

83

production team, camera crew and all their equipment were crowded into half of it, but Mike could imagine that, empty and unlit, it would be a scary room. He thought it had an odd atmosphere, quite unlike the gloom of the rest of the house; it was large, high-ceilinged, soberly decorated and expensively furnished.

There was a bright red stain on the carpet.

Clive positioned him on the floor with Jack standing over him, a long, bloody kitchen knife in his hand. Jack gave Mike a friendly wink, and Mike tried to smile back. This awful room . . .

It was grand but somehow horrible, as if it were tainted with something stale and rank. His stomach ached with hunger, but he was used to that. If this barmy old toff came back with some dough, he'd go straight to the shop and buy some fish and chips. Or a hot pie and peas . . . It was a weird place, all right. Look at those shadows crawling across the ceiling like lost souls, he'd be out of here quick as a flash, soon as he'd got his money, see if he wasn't . . .

Mike began to sweat in the heat of the lights. A make-up girl dabbed at his face and sprinkled more blood. Clive was earnestly discussing a final detail with the cameraman; the air was thick and the carpet smelled musty.

"Relax, Mike, you're supposed to be dead!" called Clive. "Close your eyes. That's better. Quiet, please . . ."

Relax, *relax*, you're supposed to be dead. Relax, relax, you're *supposed to be dead* . . . In the blind silent seconds that followed, the words resounded in his head to the irregular beating of his heart, fast and loud, like some idiot nursery chant. There were other murmurings too, indistinct and sinister, as though the voices of Jack Hatchbury's madness lived on, whispering evil through that room. Mike could hardly breathe . . .

"Cut! Splendid. Once more for luck!"

After what seemed like an age, Mike's work was over for the day. He and Bill were taken back to the television studios where he showered and changed, and then they made their way to the hotel that had been booked for them. They did not speak much. The strange, stifling effect of the room aside, Mike was always quiet after a performance; not sad exactly, but drained. Bill seemed to understand and didn't chat to him, though he himself was full of his exciting day.

At the hotel, Mike began slowly to unwind. He phoned his parents and told them about the scenes they'd shot, and then Bill took him to the restaurant and ordered dinner.

"I really enjoyed today," he said. "All those film people—you'd think they were just standing around, wouldn't you? But I was watching them, and each person's concentrating very hard on his own particular job, making sure that everything goes like clockwork . . . You're very quiet, Mike. Is anything wrong? Something on your mind?"

"It's that house, Uncle Bill," said Mike hesitantly, "Or rather, the room where we were filming this afternoon. It has a peculiar 'feel', almost as though Jack Hatchbury's influence is still there . . . It gives me the creeps."

His uncle frowned. "I'm not sure what you mean, Mike."

"Well . . . it's hard to describe, but when I'm acting I have to imagine myself into the character, think about how he'd feel and behave, right? But in that room, I didn't have to act. It's as if Tommy Briggs was there with me, as if . . . almost as if I *am* Tommy Briggs."

His uncle stared at him incredulously.

"Do you think the place is haunted?"

"No, not full of ghosts. It's more like . . ." He struggled to find the right words. "It's as if the wickedness, the madness of Jack Hatchbury lingers on in that room though Jack Hatchbury's dead. Still existing, waiting for . . ."

"For what?"

"I don't know." Mike shrugged helplessly. "It's just a feeling I've got. Maybe it's me. Maybe *I'm* going crackers."

"That's just silly!" His uncle reached across the table and patted his shoulder. "Do you know what I think? You've got too much imagination, lad! This part means a lot to you, doesn't it? You've been caught up in the story of Tommy Briggs' murder. I should never have let Jack describe it in that vivid way he has—all actors love a bit of melodrama. Well, I can tell you that I thought the room was perfectly ordinary, and I bet Jack agrees with me. Granted it's gloomy, but what old, neglected house isn't?"

"I suppose so," said Mike slowly. "I just have this very strong feeling that there's something wrong about that room."

"Well," sighed Bill, "'In the Shadow of the Rope' is quite a frightening series, I suppose, and I'm sorry you find the house so disturbing. But listen, Mike, there's absolutely no need to work if you don't want to, especially in your school holidays. If all this is upsetting you we can go home right now."

"Oh, no, of course not!" Mike was horrified at the very idea. Professionals didn't walk out on a job and let everybody down; besides, he knew nobody would ever employ him again if he did. "You're probably quite right, Uncle Bill. It's just that I've never been anywhere with such a strange sort of atmosphere."

"I'll tell you what," said his uncle, "it's been a tiring day, so we'll have a chocolate mousse to finish with, and an early night, and we'll see how you feel in the morning."

"That's fine by me." His uncle's calm common sense made Mike feel much easier. Perhaps he had been over-imaginative; he hated working in that room, but, after all, he only had one more day there.

The next morning he felt much brighter. After breakfast he and Bill went straight to the television studios. In the Wardrobe Department he was dressed in his costume, which had been freshly cleaned and dirtied, and in make-up his transformation into Tommy Briggs was completed.

They arrived on location in good time for Mike's mid-morning call. The team had started work early and were drinking coffee in the kitchen. Chrissie chatted to Bill while Clive took Mike through the script for their last day's filming.

"Tommy follows Jack into the front room and Jack tells him to wait. He goes into the kitchen and hides a knife under his coat. Meanwhile Tommy's gazing round the posh room, very impressed. There's a dark shadow in the doorway—Jack returns, and Tommy holds out his hand eagerly for his pennies. Then he sees the maniacal look on Jack's face; he's terrified. Jack produces the knife, raises it and stabs Tommy.

"We've filmed some of this already, Mike," he continued. "So what we need to do now is these shots with you: Tommy following Jack; looking round the room; holding out his hand when Jack returns; a closeup of Tommy's terrified look, and lastly, the stabbing. O.K.?"

"Yes, I understand," Mike said confidently.

Their coffee break over, the team made their way to the front room to start work. As he entered it, Mike was aware of a strange, echoing silence, as though noisy voices had suddenly been hushed. Stupid imagination, he told himself, and all but marched on to the set. Bill found a corner at the back of the room, and Chrissie sat on a chair at the side with her stopwatch and clipboard, ready to time the shots. Mike noticed that tracks had been laid on the carpet for the camera, which was mounted on a dolly, to run along. Clive showed him his "spot", the place marked with coloured floor tape where he was to stand throughout, talked him through the sequence and then went to confer with the cameraman.

Jack joined him. He was as friendly as usual but, Mike thought, a little tense: during the first rehearsal they managed to get everything wrong.

"Loosen up, Mike. You're not being forced into the room, you know!" said Clive. "And Jack, you're overdoing the stiff walk. Hatchbury had arthritis in his left knee, but he didn't move like a robot! That's better. Try it again, please."

They filmed the first scenes of Jack and Tommy walking into the room, and then of Jack returning. Both were long tracking shots, the camera being wheeled along to follow their movements, then it dollied in closer to film Tommy gazing round the luxurious room.

The filming didn't take long and, once they'd started, it wasn't difficult. By now both of them knew exactly how their characters would behave in any situation. It wasn't until they shot his close-up that Mike's fears returned. Jack towered over him with a professional scowl on his face.

Gawd, look at him! What have I done! He's lost his marbles, that's what! He's—

Stop it!

The camera captured a look of genuine terror in Mike's eyes.

"Cut. Thank you, that was fine. Take ten minutes' break, everyone." Clive drew Mike to one side. "Are you

O.K., Mike? You look a bit pale. If you'd like a proper break we can have our lunch hour now, but I thought we might push on with the last shot and wrap early—how do you feel?"

"I'd rather get on with it, thanks, Clive," said Mike. The sooner I'm finished with this place the better, he thought.

"Good lad."

Chrissie appeared with welcome cups of coffee for them.

"It's looking great from where I'm sitting," she said. "There's a marvellous atmosphere between you and Jack. Very convincing, aren't they, Clive?"

"They're frightening me to death," the director said, grinning. "Excuse me, I must just go and have a row with my cameraman."

"They're great friends really," said Chrissie. "Hello, we've lost Bill."

Mike's uncle was absorbed in conversation with the sound recordist. He caught Mike's eye and mouthed, "All right?" Mike nodded and smiled back.

"This next shot is going to remind Clive of old times," Chrissie remarked. "He started his working life as a stunt arranger. Oh good, we're getting somewhere at last, look."

Clive and the cameraman had finally agreed on the camera angle, and Jack was rehearsing a downward sweep with a long steel knife, making the blade flash dramatically in the lights. Jack concealed the knife in his coat and stood motionless and remote, waiting to begin. Clive appropriated Chrissie's chair and set it next to the camera to get a better view of the shot.

"All we're after in this shot is the back of your head, Jack's face and the glint of the knife. Then we cut, so there's no need for you to move, Mike," the director told him. "The idea is that on the screen there will be a quick fade to black on the sound of the thud of the knife, and then we'll see the shot we did yesterday, Jack standing over Tommy's dead body. Clear?"

Mike nodded and tried to relax. The atmosphere was becoming more intense, more oppressive. He thought he could hear, above the chatter in the room, a vague, insidious murmuring. He shuddered in spite of the warmth; every instinct was telling him that in this room the whispering, invisible forces of evil lingered, creeping in the carpet, scuttering silently into corners, infesting the walls. Couldn't anyone else sense it? Or was it all in his mind.

Mike closed his eyes.

"Just once more, Jack," Clive said. "Raise the knife—hold it—now! Not too fast. Try it again . . . Fine. Look up at him, Mike. Right, we'll go for a take. Turn over . . ."

Mike raised his eyes unwillingly to Jack's face, and what he saw froze him with horror. The actor's eyes were wild and glaring with malignant fury; he was rigid with tension, contorted like some monstrous machine, and suddenly Mike knew that the brain behind those eyes had snapped, that the evil voices were curled into Jack's mind like tapeworms and he no longer knew himself from the mad murderer of long ago. Mike tried to move, to speak, but terror mesmerised him.

". . . And, action!"

The knife glinted in the powerful lights and was still for an instant. But the actor hadn't finished. Suddenly galvanised, Jack sprang towards Mike like a rabid animal. The crew might have been watching from behind fifty layers of glass; as if from years away he heard the cameraman's warning yell, Chrissie screaming, the director's chair overturning as he leapt to his feet.

Cut.

JOPLIN'S

Brian Mooney

"I THINK THAT I'll go out and pick some blackberries this afternoon, my dear," said Mr. Burton, lowering his binoculars and turning to his wife, who was clearing away the lunch debris.

"That sounds nice," agreed Mrs. Burton with a vague smile. "Where will you go—down to the river bank?"

"No, all the bushes there are stripped bare," mourned Mr. Burton. "Those people from the new estate—they turn their wretched children loose just as soon as the berries start to change colour. No, I thought that I'd take a stroll up that hill over there." He indicated the place which dominated the view from their kitchen window. "That's one place I haven't been since we've lived here. I've just been taking a look through my field glasses, and I'm sure that the top is covered with brambles. There seems to be an old hut up there, too. Probably derelict, but I'd like to have a look at it."

"I always say fruit tastes so much better when it's free," his wife said with a smile. "And they won't be smothered with all that nasty insecticide. I swear that's what caused Mother's rheumatism." She thought for a moment. "Tell you what—while you're out I'll pop down to the shops and get some nice cooking apples. Then if you can get plenty of blackberries we'll have a pie, and a crumble, and I'll make some jam. You've always liked blackberry and apple jam."

"Jolly good," approved Mr. Burton, lighting his pipe and puffing away comfortably. "I'll start as soon as I've helped with the washing up. I'll take Rupert with me—I vow that dog's getting lazier each day."

The elderly clumber spaniel lying torpid in front of the gas stove wagged his tail idly at the sound of his name. Since his master's retirement he had been treated to more daily walks than he considered good for himself. Perhaps if he pretended to be asleep . . .

As soon as Mr. Burton had dried the last dish, he said that there was no time like the present and called Rupert. "Now you be sure to wrap up well," fussed Mrs. Burton. "It's terribly blustery out today, and I don't want you coming down with a chill."

"Don't you worry yourself, old girl," scoffed Mr. Burton. "Tough as they come, that's me." Still, he put on his gumboots and a comfortable muffler in addition to his anorak and floppy old hat. Didn't want to give the good lady any cause for concern.

Mrs. Burton handed him a small black plastic bucket. "This should be ideal," she told him. "Just you get that filled up and we'll have a feast."

Rupert dragging reluctantly at his heels, Mr. Burton slammed the gate shut behind him and strode off down the road. Although from the kitchen window his destination looked close, he knew that he would have to walk about a mile or so by road before he reached it. His military-style moustache bristled as he breathed in deeply through his nose. Taste that air! By Jove, this was the life. He'd always been determined to retire to the country, and fortunately Muriel felt the same way. How he'd ever stuck London all those years . . . Well, thinking about the size of his pension, he supposed that it had been worthwhile.

"Hello, Mr. Burton!" His reverie was interrupted

rather loudly, and beady eyes twinkled at him from a merry red face. It was Hewitt, the smallholder from whom they bought their eggs and other sundries.

"Afternoon, Mr. Hewitt," responded Burton. He would never had admitted it to anyone, least of all to himself, but he was not as fit as he had been, and the opportunity to pass the time of day was very welcome. Rupert flopped thankfully to the ground and began an unsightly investigation of his nether regions.

"How are you enjoying your retirement in our little village, eh?" enquired Hewitt. "Must be about six months now—not too dull after the big city?"

"Not at all," said Mr. Burton jovially. "Marvellous place. Been feeling like a youngster since I've been here." He remembered how his back twinged sometimes, and added, "Well, not exactly a youngster, but pretty fit."

"Ah, it's a good old place, this," acknowledged Hewitt. "My family's been in these parts for donkey's years." He eyed the plastic bucket curiously. "Just stretching your legs, are you?"

"Partly," said Mr. Burton, holding up the bucket. "Thought I'd get some blackberries."

"Good idea—nothing like fresh blackberries with a bit of apple and cream. But you're going the wrong way for the river bank—that's where most folk in the village go for their blackberries."

"Oh, I'm not going to the river," said Mr. Burton. "I'm taking a walk up that hill. I've not been up there yet, and it looks quite rich in brambles."

Hewitt's jolliness evaporated when he saw where Mr. Burton was pointing. Frowning, he said, "Wouldn't advise that, Mr. Burton."

"Oh, private property, is it?" asked Mr. Burton.

"Well, not exactly, it ain't . . ." said Hewitt uncertainly.

93

Mr. Burton looked puzzled. "I don't understand. Either it's privately owned or it's common land."

"Hard to say . . . it is and it ain't . . ." Hewitt scratched his head and looked a bit embarrassed. "You see, that there's Joplin's, that's what it is . . ."

"I'm sorry, Mr. Hewitt, you've quite lost me," confessed Mr. Burton. "What is er, Joplin's, I think you said?"

"Ar . . . hill used to belong to a fellow called Joplin. Bit of unpleasantness around here, and Joplin disappeared. Didn't have any heirs, so in time the place became accepted as common land. But ain't nobody from round here goes up there . . . not ever . . ."

"Why?" asked Mr. Burton.

Hewitt shifted uncomfortably and began to suck on a battered old briar pulled from his pocket. At last he muttered, "There's somethin' nasty up there, maybe . . ." He caught the look of amused scorn on Mr. Burton's face and added hastily, "Not that I'm saying there's anything in it . . . It's just that us locals prefer to steer clear of Joplin's."

Now Mr. Burton, for all his pompous manner, was a kind-hearted man and was slightly discomfited at the thought that he might have upset Hewitt, whom he considered to be a decent fellow. He offered the smallholder his tobacco pouch, and when both pipes were going to their owners' satisfaction, Mr. Burton said, "I'd like to hear the story, Mr. Hewitt."

Hewitt nodded. "Beardy Joplin, some called him, on account of he just let his beard grow wild without trimming it. And others called him Leggy Joplin, because he'd got these great long arms and legs, completely out of proportion to his body. Right miserable old sod, he were, real vicious like . . ."

94

"You knew him?" asked Mr. Burton.

"No, Leggy were before my dad's time, but my grandad knew him . . . Many's the time he told us about old Leggy Joplin and his ways. Fair put the cows off their grazing, he would."

"You said there was some unpleasantness," prompted Mr. Burton.

"That's right . . . Well, old Joplin was right jealous of that there bit of land. You can see that it'd be damn all use to anybody for anything, not even for keeping a few sheep or goats on, but Leggy Joplin was like that old fairytale . . . now what am I thinking of?"

"The dog in the manger?" suggested Mr. Burton.

"That's right!" said Hewitt, grinning. "Just like that, was Joplin. Place weren't of use to him, and he couldn't abide the thought of anybody else getting anything out of it. Anyway, one day he caught a couple of village lads up there, picking blackberries. The old devil nigh beat them to death—put them both in the cottage hospital for a good spell."

He stared up at the hill while relighting his pipe. "Well, in those days, the nearest policeman was at Patchytt, good ten miles from here. Besides, folks round here like to sort out their own problems. Real good neighbours, but tough and independent like. So some of the dads and uncles and big brothers, and some others, they took out after Leggy Joplin. They caught up with him near that there hill.

"Now it might not look much from here, but there's quite a lot of land atop that hill—a large, squarish area fully covered in brambles. Old Leggy took off up the hill as if Old Nick himself was after him. So most of the blokes in that—well, lynching party, I guess you could call it — most of them spread in a big circle round the bottom of the hill so that Leggy couldn't escape, and some others went up after him. They was gone quite a long time, and when they came down they was quiet and subdued like. Told the others they'd roughed Joplin up some, and he'd seen the error of his ways." Hewitt paused and spat into the long grass on the verge of the road.

"Well, that was the last anyone seen of Leggy Joplin. Some reckoned that he'd sneaked back down when the coast was clear and pushed off for good. But there was others as reckoned he'd never come down, that he'd been killed up on the hill that night and the lads had buried him up there. Only them as had been up the hill knew for sure, and they weren't saying nothing."

"And that's why local people shun the spot?" chuckled Mr. Burton.

Hewitt shook his head gravely. "There's a bit more to it than that," he said. "After Leggy had been gone for a few years, a local ne'er-do-well called Ratty Syme went up there to stake his claim. He never came back. A search party went looking for him, but they never found a trace. Them old brambles up there are like a tropical jungle, see? And there've been others . . . three or four maybe . . . all disappeared . . . In the end folk steered clear of Joplin's."

"And when did all this happen?" enquired Mr. Burton.

"Well, let me see . . . My grandad was just a nipper at the time, and he's been dead for quite some years, God rest him. Guess it must have been upwards of a hundred years ago."

Mr. Burton tamped down the tobacco in his pipe and struck a match. "So, nobody's been up to Joplin's for what . . . about eighty to ninety years?"

"About right," conceded Hewitt.

"Then a little bit of local history," said Mr. Burton firmly, "with several alternative and logical explanations,

96

has become a myth. And because of this myth, people have stayed clear of that land for ninety-odd years."

Hewitt nodded unhappily. He didn't seem to like the determined note in Mr. Burton's voice.

"Then I think that the time has come to lay the myth," concluded Mr. Burton.

"Look, you're a nice chap, Mr. Burton, with a nice wife and a nice old dog to care for," pleaded Hewitt. "Why cause grief by stirring up things best left alone? Now if you was to go down to the river, why, you'd collect all the blackberries you need. Wait, tell you what—there's a few brambles in a corner of my bit of land, and you're welcome to help yourself from them any time."

Mr. Burton clapped Hewitt on the shoulder. "Thanks, old chap," he boomed, "but I'm not one to be scared off by things that go bump in the night. I think that I'll get a nice crop of blackberries from Joplin's. Come along, Rupert!"

"You'll not get that old dog to go up there!" Hewitt shouted after him. "Animals have got sense . . . whole lot more sense than some folk, I reckon!"

"Inbreeding," Mr. Burton told himself as Joplin's hill loomed nearer. "That and insularity. That's the trouble with country people. They become stupid and narrow-minded and too superstitious by half . . ."

Soon he found a stile by the side of the road, and beyond it an overgrown path leading to the hill. Mr. Burton clambered over the stile and Rupert wriggled under the lowest bar. "That's a good boy," Mr. Burton praised the dog. "We'll show 'em, won't we Rupert?"

A walk of about a hundred yards, impeded slightly by the long grass, brought the pair to the foot of the hill. Suddenly Rupert sat down and began to whimper. "Heel, Rupert!" Mr. Burton called sternly. Rupert just whined.

Mr. Burton walked back to him, speaking sharply. The old spaniel leaned against his master's leg, and to Mr. Burton's astonishment the dog was trembling violently.

"We can well do without this nonsense!" Mr. Burton admonished the animal. Picking the dog up with some difficulty, he began to ascend the hill. Rupert started to struggle desperately. As soon as Mr. Burton put him down, the dog turned and made rapidly for the stile, expending more energy than he had in years. By the time Mr. Burton had reached the stile, the clumber spaniel was well down the road, galloping furiously towards home and ignoring Mr. Burton's angry shouts.

After one last, futile bellow, Mr. Burton stamped grimly back to the base of the hill. "Be damned if I'll waste my afternoon!" he snorted as he started to climb for the second time.

The hill was fairly small as hills go, but it was steep, and Mr. Burton had to pause several times to catch his breath on the way up. At last he reached the summit and turned to look back the way that he had come. The road and the patchwork of fields and the village were spread out before him. Now where was it . . .? Ah yes, there was his house, recognisable by its green-tiled roof. He wondered if that fool dog had got home yet. Hope the wife wouldn't be worried when she saw that the dog was alone. But no, she was going shopping for apples, wasn't she?

Mr. Burton surveyed the top of the hill. As Hewitt had said, it was surprisingly large, covered by a mass of thick brambles with just a few natural spaces meandering between the bushes. In the distance he could make out the gimcrack roof of the old shack, jutting above the tangled bushes. The brambles glistened with huge, juicy-looking blackberries, and Mr. Burton sighed happily. Why should some silly, local superstition bother him? After all, the foolishness of the villagers had just handed him his very own private bramble patch.

He knew what he'd do—he'd fill the bucket to the brim so he could present some of the berries to Hewitt. Good sort, Hewitt, and he'd probably have a good chuckle over his silliness. Mr. Burton struck into the thickets.

For some time he collected blackberries in plenty, although he found the going far from easy. The brambles were old and thick and tangled, spreading their arms at low level across the path, often concealed by the long grass. Mr. Burton was very grateful for the protection afforded by his gumboots. And then as he was reaching—straining almost, for although he was a fairly tall man, the choicest berries seemed perversely determined to stay just beyond his reach—as he was reaching for a particularly succulent fruit, he saw the spider.

Mr. Burton stooped to look at the spider. He had always been interested in natural history and rather prided himself on his knowledge of wildlife. But this spider was quite unlike any that he had seen before: however, as there are some six hundred species of spider in Britain, that was hardly surprising.

It was squatting upside down in the centre of a web not unlike that built by a garden spider, but garden spider it was not. Its body was larger for one thing, and its gangling, almost disproportionate, legs covered a far greater spread. It seemed as if it was watching Mr. Burton, and it had a sinister air about it.

Then the spell was broken. A careless fly hit the web obliquely and the spider pounced on its prey. Mr. Burton straightened up and breathed out, as if in relief. "Don't be silly," he scolded himself. "It's just a spider. Interesting marks on its back, though. Reminds me of something — can't think what . . ."

Mr. Burton plunged deeper into the brambles. He noticed how strong the wind had become. Sudden whipping gusts lashed at him, while lighter breezes wafted the branches and berries away from his questing hand, compelling him to stretch, to struggle harder against the brambles. He'd collected a number of scratches, including a rather deep one on the back of his right hand, which was bleeding freely.

Mr. Burton's heart jumped. He had almost touched another of those spiders, again sitting in the middle of a web. Mr. Burton had never thought of any wildlife as evil, but yes—the spider looked evil. This one was perched head uppermost, and Mr. Burton peered closely at it. Suddenly it struck him what those markings brought to mind. They seemed to form the face of an old man, an unpleasant old man with a long and wiry beard.

The spider began to vibrate its web furiously, as will a garden spider when it feels threatened. Despite the cold wind, Mr. Burton felt a sweat break out on his forehead. Those long legs, those markings . . . a bearded face . . . Beardy Joplin . . . Leggy Joplin . . .

"Stop it, you damned old fool!" Mr. Burton swore at himself. "You've let that stupid story get to you!" He took several deep breaths in an effort to calm down. Then he knew what to do. He had a friend who was an arachnologist at Regent's Park Zoo. He'd capture this spider, take it home in a matchbox and send it to his friend for identification. He reached out, hand still trembling slightly.

Something flopped on to the back of his hand. It was yet another spider of the same species, rather larger than those he had seen so far. Mr. Burton gave a startled cry and attempted to dislodge the creature. It clung to him, and to his horror it seemed to be lapping at the blood

It clung to him . . .

pouring from the deep scratch. Almost hysterical, he swept at it with his left hand and it bit him savagely. A fiery, molten pain shot through his arm.

"*You brute!*" cried Mr. Burton, crushing the spider with a blow. Somehow he brushed against the web and received a second bite from its occupant. In agony he tumbled down and forward into the bush, sharp thorns tearing at his face. He felt the sting of a third spider. As he crouched there moaning, Mr. Burton noticed that a tiny path breaking the brambles led straight to the door of the ramshackle building where Joplin had lived. Mr. Burton hadn't realised how far he had strayed. "Must get in there," he mumbled. "Shelter . . ."

Mr. Burton heaved himself upright, and his flailing foot kicked over the almost-full bucket of blackberries. He lurched towards the shack and wrenched open its rotting door. A croak of mingled fear and disgust burst from his lips when he saw what was inside.

The floor of the hut had burst upwards in a mad confusion of brambles, and from the centre of the patch a bony face leered wildly at Mr. Burton. The gangling limbs of the remains were draped in mouldering scraps of clothing, and the tattered remnants of an unkempt beard clung to the skull. The posture of the thing was such that it appeared to be enthroned. A crazy thought occurred to Mr. Burton. "The King of the Castle," he giggled.

Other spiders were now attacking Mr. Burton as he retreated from the hut. Needle fangs struck once, twice, and again . . . Mr. Burton's body was racked with hurt and the spines of the bushes ripped at him. The jaws of the skull seemed spread in maniacal laughter.

Mr. Burton's ankle caught in a bramble, and the strong wind knocked him from his feet into the midst of another thicket behind him. He cried out, terror-stricken, as more spiders injected him with their burning poison. And then it seemed to him that a giant hand reached into his chest and crushed his heart. Breath exploded from him in a mortal scream.

Just before Mr. Burton died, he discovered that he was not alone in the bramble thicket. Scattered around him in the undergrowth were several sets of whitened and strangely pitted bones, and it seemed to his dimming eyes that the brambles were already knitting themselves more closely about him . . .

The spiders continued to swarm from the brambles towards Mr. Burton's body, until they were so thickly clustered as to be almost indistinguishable from the shiny mass of spilled blackberries.

THE SHAFT

Phillip C. Heath

GARY LAY IN the warm darkness of his room and listened reflectively to "taps" being played outside in the courtyard below. Beneath him, in the bottom bunk, his roommate listened also.

"Hey, I was just thinking," Tom said in a low voice. "You really think we can trust Billingsley—count on him, I mean?"

"He'll do all right." Then, as an afterthought: ". . . He'd better, if he knows what's good for him."

A few minutes of silence intervened before again Tom stirred and leaned out from the edge of his bunk. "How long you figure we oughta wait?" he asked a bit impatiently, nervously.

"Let's give it a half-hour or so—at least until after bed-check."

Gary heard his friend roll back and settle into bed. A short time later there were other noises, further down the hall . . . the faint voices of two of their superior officers, and a soft opening and closing of doors as the pair went from room to room making certain everyone was present and accounted for. At length the familiar footsteps approached their own room, and abruptly the door eased open a crack to reveal within two shadowy figures in bed, obviously fast asleep, considering their deep, rhythmic breathing.

The door quietly clicked shut and the footsteps echoed away into the long empty silence of the corridor beyond.

Tom gave a short sigh of relief. Gary remained motionless, letting the plan replay itself on the dark screen of his mind.

They'd found it two days ago, Saturday morning, while cleaning out the trunkroom, a storage place for trunks, suitcases, travel bags and the like. In an obscure corner of the ceiling Gary had by chance noticed a small, square trapdoor. Curious, he pushed it back out of the way, using the handle of his broom, and with the aid of a folding chair was able to shimmy up and pull himself through. The opening led into a sizeable section of the building's attic. Yet prowling about in the unaccustomed darkness brought them not only to discovery but almost to disaster as well. Another careless step and Tom would have stumbled headlong into the yawning, bottomless void of blackness at his feet.

It was the shaft.

The event was rather like happening upon some long-lost legend, finding this old elevator shaft. The building, "D Barracks" as it was called, dated back to the 1840s. At that time there had been in use, for the privilege of officers, an old-fashioned pulley-type lift or elevator. But it seemed that through the years a number of sinister accidents directly led to the deaths of four students. Eventually the elevator was condemned as being more or less unsafe, and after its removal the entire area was permanently closed off. Nevertheless, a stray, fanciful rumour still managed on occasion to drift down from grade to grade: something to the effect that the shaft was cursed—haunted. Of course, the two boys generally held such talk as nonsense, but it certainly served to add a delicious shiver to the adventure at hand. And in a Missouri military school so rare an adventure as this was hard to come by.

Since it was near the end of term, the trunkroom had been eagerly emptied out and left unlocked. With even a little caution they could come and go as they pleased, unhindered and unnoticed. But it was the discovery of the rope that first kindled the idea of actually descending into the depths of the shaft: a heavy length of hemp, about three centimetres in diameter, firmly knotted through a pulley fastened to a crossbeam above. Surprisingly enough, it showed only slight evidence of ageing, and still proved quite strong.

The next day, Sunday afternoon, had been the trial run. The floor had been relatively deserted, with almost everyone gone into town. The snackroom was closed, too—for that was where the shaft seemed to lead . . . past the dormitory and classroom storeys, straight down to the ground floor, specifically the rear kitchen area of a large snack bar where the students spent a good deal of their leisure time, playing pinball and video games in the adjoining games room. This bottom portion of the shaft had long ago been converted into a sort of cupboard, a place to store extra or broken chairs, but it hadn't been used for years and apparently was all but forgotten. This was probably why the two boys found the door at the bottom of the shaft unlocked.

But even though it had looked pretty dark inside the kitchen, it was altogether much too risky to try entering during the day. And this led to Gary's mischievous plan that they return the following night, sneak in and pay a brief visit to the snack bar—perhaps switch on a video game or two.

So that was where Billingsley fitted in. They needed someone to play sentry, and warn them should some officer wander by at an inopportune time. Although Billingsley was a mealy-mouthed sissy who always found something to complain about, he wouldn't dare foul up their plan. Yes, the plan . . .

Gary looked at the glowing numbers of the digital alarm clock on his desk. Almost eleven-fifteen. It was time.

"Tom—you ready?"

A creak from the bunk below. "Ready as I'll ever be."

Silently they slipped into their clothes and crept out to the passage. Everything was dark, still, and quiet. They moved noiselessly to Billingsley's room and tapped on the door.

When there was no answer, Gary stuck his head inside. "Psst—Billingsley! You awake?"

A frail, pale-looking boy, half-asleep, mumbled something and got dressed. He joined them out in the corridor, closing the door behind him.

"Your roommate still asleep?" Tom asked.

"Yeah."

Gary broke in. "C'mon, then. This way."

They followed him to the trunkroom, where he turned and whispered his orders once more to Billingsley. "Now remember, stay here just inside the door, and if you hear anyone coming let us know right away, then hide, just in case. Got it?"

"Yeah," came the toneless reply.

Gary gave him one of the walkie-talkies Tom had managed to sneak from the supply room. The other he fixed to his belt, and after one last check to make sure they had everything, he climbed up into the attic. Tom handed him their only flashlight, then clambered up behind him.

It was as black as black could ever be. Gary flicked on the light and let its ghostly amber beam flit about until it fell upon the shaft. They walked carefully over to it.

The light feebly plumbed the depths, frightening the

shadows deeper. It was like some terrible abyss falling forever, perhaps to the very bowels of the earth, or even hell. But no, it did not. They had already once ventured to its bottom. This would be no different. Yet even as they told themselves this, they knew otherwise. It had been dismal enough by day; it was not difficult to guess what it might be like at night. Gary found it painfully easy to imagine cockroaches as long as a grown man's finger, big, fat-bellied rates, and no telling what else. And that brought to mind an eerie bit of history concerning the shaft. The building had been built on a piece of land next to a desolate graveyard no longer in use, dating back some time before the turn of the century. It was said that when workmen were digging the basement below the kitchen, they uncovered an alarming number of bones. Although never really disclosed as to whether animal or human, it was generally assumed they weren't animal. As for how they had come to be there, outside the established perimeter of the cemetery . . . well, that remained something of a mystery.

Of course, many theories were secretly exchanged, but the important discovery came when a deep fissure was located somewhere beneath the subsoil. Excavation was brought to a halt with the basement only half completed, for fear further digging might lead to a gradual weakening of the building's foundation. However, it was hinted that the real reason was deliberately hushed up . . . something about the fissure being likened to a subterranean tunnel or burrow of some sort. At any rate, the full length of the shaft leading to the basement had been made inaccessible by blocking if off with floorboards at ground level, where it adjoined the kitchen area. The tales eventually played themselves out, and no one dwelt on the subject these days. It had all been long forgotten. Almost.

A hand was suddenly laid upon Gary's shoulder. "What's the matter?" Tom sounded worried. "Anything wrong?"

Gary looked up from his thoughts. "No, nothing. I guess I was just thinking about something."

"You . . . you wanna . . . call it off?"

The question snapped him fully back to the present. "I'll go first," he answered flatly.

Tom took over the flashlight and held it on his friend, who stepped to the edge of the great black mouth, briefly hesitated, and started down. The descent wasn't too difficult. Whenever he grew tired he paused momentarily at each floor, balancing himself on the narrow ledge every ten feet or so. The only real problem was with the end of the rope, which swayed back and forth to bump noisily against the sides of the shaft. But that couldn't be helped.

It took him a little longer to reach the bottom this time, because the darkness demanded a certain degree of caution. Everything was very dirty; dust disturbed by his activity arose all around him in thick grey clouds. The air was oppressively warm and stifling, and smelled strangely unpleasant. He was unable to suppress a quick shudder before signalling Tom to lower the flash light. This was dropped to him on a long length of cord. Then Tom got a grip on the rope and made his way down.

They both stood amid a helter-skelter jumble of old chairs stacked upside-down on one another, their legs sticking up every which way like stiff hairs on a monster's back. The two turned their attention towards the door leading to the dark, empty kitchen. Tom poised the flashlight on the door handle. They held each other's gaze for an instant in the gloom, then Gary slowly, quietly turned the knob and pushed it inward.

But something was wrong. The door did not open, save for a thin crack. It was being held by—

A chain! A metal chain guard near the upper portion of the door on the other side prevented them from entering. Evidently someone in the kitchen had recently slid it into place—or else they simply hadn't noticed it the first time. After all, they had only opened to door enough to observe that it was unlocked.

Both boys slumped in utter discouragement. To have come so far, planned and gone to so much trouble, only to be rudely turned back by a single brass chain. Still, Gary supposed, there was somewhere deep down inside them a tiny spark of relief. If they had been caught . . .

But there were other things to worry about now—like getting out of this awful place as soon as possible. Tom wasted little time in starting back up. Gary held the flashlight for him, climbing on top of the pile to offer as much light as possible. Tom was scarcely ten feet over his head when all at once one of the chairs on whch Gary stood tilted crazily and sent him tumbling backwards to the floor below. Several of the other chairs clattered down on top of him. The flashlight rolled into a corner.

Tom hurried back down the rope. "Gary! You O.K.?" His voice was somewhat shaky.

Gary tried to stir but winced in pain. "My—my arm . . . I think it's broken." It was twisted behind him, pinned down by his own weight.

For a moment Tom just stood there stupidly, not quite knowing what to do, when suddenly a familiar voice crackled over the walkie-talkie on his belt.

"Fellers? This is me . . . I can hear someone down the hall, comin' this way. I—I'm goin' back to my room before I get caught—" *Click.* Silence.

Tom snatched up the transceiver. "Billingsley! Don't go, we need you!"

"Too late," Gary muttered slowly, through clenched teeth. "He's gone. The little jerk. He'll catch it for this. Probably just someone going along to the bathroom."

Tom turned back to stare at him with wide, dismayed eyes. "Y-You O.K. for now? Does it hurt bad?"

"Not too much, except when I try to move . . . but—"

"Then I'm gonna get help. Hang on."

And he began scrambling hurriedly up the rope.

"No—wait!" Gary called after him. "Get this stuff offa me!"

But Tom was already almost half way up.

Gary watched from the deep gloom at the bottom of the shaft as his friend made his way higher, higher, until—

Somewhere far overhead there was the sharp snap of metal, then a quick, shrill cry of terror—and he watched in helpless horror as Tom came plunging down, down out of the darkness far above him, flailing his arms wildly in the empty air, crashing heavily upon the upthrust legs of the chairs. A second later the big steel pulley knifed a whistling descent as it and the slack rope splintered through the wooden seat of a chair hardly a foot away from his own head.

When Gary at last dared open his eyes he saw his friend silhouetted in the dim light, his bloody, broken body sprawled out grotesquely among the fingerlike legs of the chairs. Gary frantically called to him, but the only answer was a faint groan. At least Tom was still alive.

Then the smashed flashlight flickered and went out, and Gary was immediately thrust back into a realm of shadow; of confinement, cobwebs, and filth. The shaft had devoured him.

For many long minutes he lay there, his guts all numb

and cold, the horrible vision of the fall repeating itself over and over again in the blackness before him. Finally it was crowded out by other thoughts that began to run rampant in his head. The creeping fear, the despair, the blind panic . . .

Just then a large spider scurried across his cheek, and he let out a short shriek. His frenzied effort to throw off the weight holding him down caused a sharp pain to shoot up his arm, sending a rush of blood to his brain that made him dizzy and nauseous. Moaning, he fell back and lay still again. After a while he tried calling for help, but his voice was too weak, muffled by the thick walls of the shaft.

What seemed like an eternity was perhaps less than an hour, when suddenly he fancied he heard a noise slipping through the solemn stillness. Yes, it was close by. He tried to clear his head, orientate himself. The door. He recognised now an indistinct murmur of what sounded like voices coming from the other side of the door, in the kitchen. His heartbeats shook him. Oh, Billingsley! he wanted to shout, you called someone after all. They've come to take us away from this dreadful place.

The chain was slid back, the door opened wide. Gary looked up as if out of a dream, his vision blurred by tears. Now hands were pulling him out of the shaft, to safety. The nightmare was over.

The following morning, for the fifth time, Billingsley told his story to the adult staff. And, for the fifth time, he went into great detail as to how he wanted no part of it from the beginning, and was threatened into co-operation. He was also assured once more that he would receive no punishment for his involvement.

For the first time in eighty-odd years, the shaft was

reopened, and a thorough investigation was made of the entire incident. As might have been expected, the thin wooden planking that served as the makeshift floor at ground level had slowly rotted away, allowing the chairs and everything inside to settle the remaining ten feet or so to the shaft's true bottom. Thus, it led not just to the kitchen, as supposed, but all the way to the basement. The two students, distracted and nervous and hindered by the pressing darkness, could easily have failed to notice the number of floors as they descended.

Yes, perhaps all that was to be expected. However, further examination of this lower portion of the shaft revived some old, familiar rumours. The rusted chain found on the *inside*, or basement side of the door, was puzzling enough, but no one could begin to explain the complete disappearance of the two boys . . . or the untidy pile of bones in the centre of the basement, freshly picked, like the remains of a chicken dinner.

OLD WIGGIE

Mary Danby

CENTURIES AGO, thought Susan, Miss Wigan would have been publicly denounced as a witch. If you were old or mis-shapen, lived alone and shunned the company of your neighbours, you were held to blame for everyone else's misfortunes. In a crude kind of trial, you might be ducked in the village pond. If you drowned, you were declared to be innocent. If you floated, it proved you were a witch, and they tied you to a stake on the village green and burned you alive, with all the villagers—even the children, gathering to cheer and spit on your ashes. And still the farmer's baby would be sickly, and the harvest poor and the well dried up. But the people would feel they'd had their revenge, and village life would settle back to normality.

"Do you believe in witches?" Susan had once asked her mother.

"Not really," her mother had replied, "though they say there are still some people around who practise witchcraft. They make their spells, and hold secret meetings, but I don't think they have any real power, whatever they might like to claim. Some of them are known as white witches. They use their so-called magic only for good purposes."

Miss Wigan wouldn't be one of those. She was evil through and through. You could tell that just by looking. She was old-ish and bent, living in a tumbledown cottage with a huge black cat. Her familiar, that would be: a representative of the devil that helped her with her spells. All witches had them. And whatever her mother said about witchcraft, Susan wasn't taking any chances—even when it was supposed to be her turn to deliver Miss Wigan's papers.

"I'm not doing Marple's Lane," she told her brother. "*You'll* have to."

"Afraid of Old Wiggie? Afraid of the witch?" taunted David, sorting out the heaps of newspapers on the kitchen table. "Afraid she'll cut you into little pieces and pop you in her cauldron?"

Susan didn't answer. She picked up the piles for Church Road and Parson's Walk and put them into her canvas bag. A few minutes later, with the bag tucked into the basket of her bicycle, she had set off on her delivery round. A *Daily Mail* for Mr. Steadman at Number Two, a *Telegraph* for the Jacksons at Number Four, *Playhour* for the vicarage children, *Woman's Own* for Mrs. Millichap . . . The morning air, cold for October, gnawed at her cheeks, and the wind tangled her long brown hair as she went from house to house, pushing papers and magazines through doors. When she had finished, there was just time for her to run home, put her bike away and grab a piece of toast before going up to the corner to wait for the school bus.

"I saw the witch this morning," David said as they stood with their hands in their pockets, stamping their feet to keep warm until the bus came.

Susan looked the other way.

"She pulled aside her cobweb curtains and fixed me with her evil eye," he went on, with a sly grin. "Then she lifted one bony, skeleton finger and beckoned to me . . . Oooh-er." He made a scary noise. Susan shrugged her

115

shoulders and, when the bus came along, went to the back to sit with her friend Georgina.

But though she would never say it in so many words — not to her brother, anyway—Susan really was afraid of the old woman in Laburnum Cottage. She had been there for about two years, living alone. All the children in the village said she was a witch, and more than one had a lurid tale to tell of hearing spells and incantations, or seeing her grinding mysterious herbs in a big stone bowl. Of course, she was probably quite harmless, just a lonely old woman who had no one to talk to but herself and who knew how to make her own herbal medicines. But Susan kept out of her way all the same, preferring not to get close enough to find out the truth.

Yesterday, when she had ridden her bicycle past the end of Marple's Lane, she had caught sight of a strange black garment left overnight on the washing line, pale and stiff with early frost. Witch clothes. A tattered cloak that would fly out behind you as you swooped over the rooftops on your broomstick. Or an old dressing-gown. Or not.

Neither David nor Susan saw Miss Wigan again for several days, although Susan, for once pushed into taking her turn down Marple's Lane, heard her talking in a high, rather silly voice to her horrible cat.

When the Ellises' tame rabbit, known as Puff, disappeared mysteriously from its hutch one day, David said rabbits' tails were a basic ingredient of all sorts of spells, everyone knew that.

That night, Susan had a dream in which she was pursued across fields by a black, leaping hag. Her ears were filled with a shrill whistling, and as she ran she floundered and stumbled, and the lights of distant houses moved with her, never growing closer. Every time she looked back in desperation over her shoulder she could see the hideous, cavorting figure, making huge hops over the ground towards her like a drunken crow, its dark old robes spread like feathered wings. It had the face of Miss Wigan.

Flap! Flap! The wings beat nearer . . .

"You left your window wide open," said Susan's mother, coming into her bedroom and catching at the wild curtains. "There's been quite a gale in the night."

On Saturdays, when the papers had to be paid for, her mother did the paper round herself, with a big leather shoulder bag to collect the money in. It wasn't that she couldn't trust David and Susan to give the right change—she enjoyed calling on everyone and exchanging the latest gossip.

On the last Saturday in October, she woke up with a sore throat and a headache.

"I feel all hot and shivery," she complained. "You had better do the paper money today, Susan."

"What about David?" argued Susan. "Why can't he do it?"

"He's got football practice. Come on, Susan, don't be difficult when I've got a headache. Put the papers in the old pram—it'll be easier than trying to manage them all on your bike."

Reluctantly, Susan picked up a pile of newspapers. She noticed the date: October 31st. Oh no. That settled it. There was no way she was going to the witch's house. Not today. Not on Hallowe'en.

She found David by the back door, putting his football boots into a bag.

"I'll give you my pocket money. Go on—you don't need to practise your football. You're really good—honest."

David made a derisory noise. "Keep your pocket money, diddums. Be a big strong girlie and brave the witch in her den." He paused. "Only . . . do be careful—her nails are long black talons that can claw the flesh off little girls' bones . . ."

"My pen with the digital clock in it—you can have that."

"Oh, you are a *wimp*, Susan," said David.

She hated him. Yet at the same time she hated herself for her silly fear. For being such a coward. Such a—yes, wimp.

She left the pram by the gate of Laburnum Cottage. Brambles caught at her from the untidy hedge. The path leading to the front door was uneven and weedy, as if visitors were not welcome. Apart from the sound of Susan's feet on the old flagstones, there was silence. No birds were singing, no cars went past the end of the lane; no children played in the woods beyond.

Laburnum Cottage was square and squat, like a crouching toad. Built of dark grey stone with a slate roof, it had no colourful creepers to soften its outline, no late roses to climb brightly against its drabness. Old green paint flaked from the window frames and doors. The curtains were grey and droopy. It was a dead place, a place of shadows and hushed whispers, the sort of place you might crawl into to die unseen. *A witch's house.*

There was no doorbell. Susan lifted her hand to the rusty doorknocker and knocked once, twice. Nothing happened for some time, then there was a shuffling sound from the hallway beyond, and slowly the door was opened.

"Yes?" Miss Wigan stared at her round the door, shrinking, as if afraid. By her side, pressed tight against her grey-stockinged leg, was her cat, an enormous, ugly, black creature with tousled fur and eyes that bored into you like yellow lasers. It spat at Susan, showing uneven teeth that seemed much too big for its mouth.

Susan drew back a little and took a breath before saying, "Paper money, please." She had decided to be businesslike. She looked straight at Miss Wigan, saw the cracked, pale skin, the pointed, cross-looking features, the protruding brown eyes. Her gaze went from the wild grey hair, home-trimmed and straggly, past the droopy cardigan and sagging skirt to the dirty pink slippers. "The paper money," Susan repeated, holding out the notebook in which her mother had written the amount.

Miss Wigan looked past her to the road. "Where are the others?" she asked in her high, witchy voice.

"What others?"

Miss Wigan appeared confused. "I don't know. I'll get my purse." She turned away, then stopped and came back. "Would you like to come inside and wait?"

Susan gaped. "Oh . . . no, no thanks."

She watched Miss Wigan shuffle down the passage into the kitchen, followed by the cat, which turned once to give Susan a nasty stare. The house was dark inside, the windows too smeared and dusty to let in much light. Wallpaper with a faded floral pattern lined the walls of the hallway, and a narrow staircase leading to the bedrooms was made even narrower by the piles of junk and old magazines that lay heaped on its steps. Was she a witch, wondered Susan, or just a poor, dotty woman who couldn't quite cope? But there was definitely something sinister about Laburnum Cottage and its inhabitant, something she couldn't quite put a finger on . . . She remembered her dream, and the black, flapping hag, and felt a chill run swiftly, teasingly through her body.

Miss Wigan poked her fierce old head round the kitchen door. "Could you help me, dear? I know I've put my purse down somewhere, but I can't seem to find it."

Looking quickly from side to side, as if seeking escape, Susan stammered, "Are you—are you sure? I'm not much good at finding things. I mean—" She knew she was gabbling, but couldn't help it—"My mother always says I'd lose my nose if it wasn't attached to me."

"Does she? How funny," said Miss Wigan in an absent-minded way. Then, remembering her problem, she said again: "Could you help me find my purse, girlie? I seem to have lost it."

Susan gave up and, taking a deep breath, crossed the threshold. The atmosphere inside the house was musty and oppressive, with a smell of old cooking and something that had gone slightly bad. Inside the kitchen, Susan was shocked to see piles of dirty saucepans on the table, and an overflowing rubbish bin.

Miss Wigan pushed the saucepans about. "It was here somewhere . . ." she muttered to herself. She picked up a cast-iron frying pan, black with burnt-on food. "Have a rummage over there, will you?" She pointed to a sideboard stacked with dishes and old newspapers.

Susan turned to look. The next moment she felt a bang on the back of her head. Falling, she clutched at a pile of plates, which crashed to the stone-flagged floor. Then somewhere inside her head someone turned off the lights.

There were parallel lines in front of her eyes. Her head throbbed painfully, and when she tried to move, it felt as though a rugby team were stamping on her brain.

"Awake?" Miss Wigan was peering at her. "That's a good girl."

As Susan opened her eyes, she saw that the parallel

lines were the bars of a big, square cage—the sort that animals sometimes travel in—which now stood in the middle of the kitchen table. Dirty saucepans had been swept to the floor to make room for it. She was sitting hunched up inside it, with her knees somewhere by her ears, and there was no room to move at all.

Gradually, the frightfulness of her bizarre situation became clear.

"What have you done?" she shouted in fear. "Let me out!" She shook the bars of the cage. "You can't *do* this! I have to go home!"

Shouting made her head hurt. More quietly, she went on, "Look, just unlock this cage, will you? You can't keep me here."

Memories of *Hansel and Gretel* came to her. The witch in the gingerbread house, imprisoning Hansel in a cage, poking at him with her finger, fattening him for the pot. "Come on," she said, beginning to panic. "Come on —you've got to let me out!"

Miss Wigan still peered happily at her. Then she bent down and picked up the great black cat.

"Here, Prince, take a look at Girlie." She put the cat next to the cage, where it sat and stared at Susan with a look of pure hate. It smelt primitive, like circus lions.

"Prince. I call him Prince. The Black Prince. The Prince of Darkness."

Suddenly, the cat stretched out a lightning-swift paw and scratched Susan's bare leg between her sock and her trouser leg.

"Ouch!"

The scratch was deep and really hurt. Blood trickled down into her sock. The cat stood up, and the tip of its tail twitched briefly before it jumped down from the table.

"I think he likes you," said Miss Wigan.

The scratch was deep . . .

"Oh, really!" Susan was now as angry as she was frightened. What right had the silly old woman to keep her here, witch or no witch.

"They'll miss me soon," she said. "The police will come and look for me, and then you'll be in trouble."

"Oh, I don't think so," said Miss Wigan, pulling a chair up to the table, right in front of the cage. "You're a big girl—they'll think you've gone to visit your friends."

"There's the pram with the papers in it—" began Susan, realizing too late that it would have been better to keep her mouth shut and hope someone would find the pram and would know where she was.

But Miss Wigan smiled, showing grey, crooked teeth, and said: "Don't worry, dear. It's quite safe. I've wheeled it round the back."

Susan's heart sank. Here she was, stuck in a cage by a total loony, unlikely to be found for hours. But the stupid old witch surely couldn't be planning to keep her here for ever. It was just a matter of sitting it out. She could do with a drink of water, but as far as she could see there was nothing in the kitchen clean enough to drink out of. A mug would do, though it might be too thick to pass between the bars. Ah, but then Old Wiggie would have to open the door of the cage . . .

"Could I have some water?"

Miss Wigan slowly got up and went to the sink, where she started to fill a grimy teapot.

Not tea, you old fool.

But she was not such an old fool. She poked the spout of the teapot between the bars.

"Drink up, then, girlie."

Susan pushed the teapot away. Her head throbbed. She wanted to stretch out her legs.

"We'll put it here for later," Miss Wigan said

comfortably, setting the teapot down on the table. "Now then, how about a little chat."

"Not unless you let me out," said Susan, thinking that the moment Miss Wigan undid the padlock, she'd be out of that house and up the lane, and telling the police, and it wouldn't be long before Old Wiggie found out for herself what it was like behind bars.

The old lady twisted her fingers together. "I so seldom have anyone to talk to," she explained, wrinkling her lined, pale forehead. "I don't have any friends, you see."

I'm not surprised, thought Susan, if you go around bashing people over the head with frying pans. She winced, as pain stabbed behind her eyes.

"I used to have friends," Miss Wigan went on. "I was in a big place where there were lots of people, and I liked some of them. Mind you—" She frowned confidentially —"Some of them were *very* peculiar. There was one man who used to go on and on about his bedsocks. Never stopped. Just bedsocks. You couldn't hold a conversation with him. Not a real one, that is, like I'm having with you."

Some conversation. More than a bit one-sided. Still, best to humour the old girl. Susan sighed loudly and shifted her weight. She could feel the beginning of cramp.

"Sylvia was nice, of course. She was my best friend. But they took her somewhere else. It was the pills. They shouldn't have given her the pills. Made her so weepy, you see."

From outside the cottage, by the gate, came loud scuffling and giggling.

"Can you see her? Is she there? Oy, are you there, Wiggie?"

"Sssh! She'll hear you."

"So? Hiya, Witchy? Want any newts' eyes today? Tongue of bat? Lizards' innards?"

Giggles all round.

"Come on, she's not listening."

Susan recognized two of the voices: Terry Weston and June Fairclough, who were in her form at school.

"Hey!" she shouted, and her voice banged in her head. "Hey! It's me, Susan! She's got me locked up! Help!"

Miss Wigan was quickly on her feet and, with sudden fury, reached through the side of the cage to grab a piece of Susan's hair. She gave a tug that nearly tore it out by the roots.

"Ow! Help, someone! No!" Susan's head was still thudding with pain, and this new torture was unbearable. Miss Wigan gave her hair another jerk, then pulled tight, holding Susan's head hard against the bars, daring her to make any more noise.

"Did you hear that?" It was Terry.

"Sort of shouting. Yes."

"Think we should look through the windows?"

"Yes. Go on. I dare you."

Yes, yes, thought Susan. Come and look—oh *please*, for God's sake come and look.

As if reading her thoughts, the old woman tugged again. Susan swallowed a yell.

"Nah. The windows are too dirty. There'd be nothing to see."

"You're scared."

"Not."

"Are."

"Not."

"Scared of Wiggie the Witch. Scared she'll put a vile spell on yer. Scared she'll turn you into a frog."

"I'm going. It was probably nothing, anyway. Race you to the end of the lane."

Susan heard them scrambling for their bicycles, then they rowdily left, pedalling up the road.

She was almost in tears.

"You see, dear?" said Miss Wigan, letting go of her hair. "That's what I have to put up with all the time. They call me a witch. That's not very nice, is it? Did you think I was a witch? Well you can see I'm not, can't you." She looked at Susan for confirmation. Susan nodded her head, terrified and lonely, now that she could no longer hear the shouts of her friends. She rubbed her scalp, where it was sore, and found there was blood on her fingers.

"Not crying, are you, dear? I won't keep you in there for long. Now, where was I? Yes, I used to tell them things, the doctors, you know, about things I'd done, but they never believed me, so then I stopped telling them those things, and they let me go and live somewhere else. Sheltered housing, they call it. It was a room in a boarding house, and the landlady was supposed to be my friend and look after me, only she never spoke to me. Well, one day I just hopped on a bus and came here. This house belonged to my Uncle William. I expect you knew him."

Susan thought she could remember a very old man who used to dig the garden and swear at passers-by over the hedge.

"They never found me, but I don't suppose they looked very hard. After all, what's one less nutcase?" Miss Wigan was twisting her face in what seemed to Susan to be anguish, but she could spare little pity for her tormentor.

"They should have kept you locked up. You're barmy," she said through her tears. "And if you don't let me out they'll send you to prison for hundreds of years. I hate you—you're a nasty, smelly old witch and I want to go *home*!" She screeched the last word, and Miss Wigan, who had been leaning forward, inspecting her, backed away suddenly.

"Very well," she said. "I can see you're not in the mood

for a chat after all. Perhaps we'd better just get on with things."

What things? Was she going to unlock the cage?

"Prince! Here, Prince!"

Why was she calling the cat?

Miss Wigan pulled at a string around her neck and produced a key from somewhere inside her musty clothes. The cat leapt on to the table and sat by the cage, glaring at Susan. Remembering the sharpness of his claws, she shrank back from the bars.

"I told you, didn't I," said Miss Wigan. "He likes the look of you."

"Let me out," Susan said sullenly, sniffing back her tears. "Let me out. Let me out."

"All in good time." Miss Wigan taunted her with the key. "First things first." She leant forward suddenly and grabbed a big hank of Susan's hair through the top of the cage, pulling it through the bars.

"Don't—" Susan began, instinctively crouching lower, but this only made it hurt more. "Ow! Don't . . . please . . . " she whimpered.

"I shan't hurt you, dear. Not if you behave," said Miss Wigan, doing something with Susan's hair—she couldn't see what. "Poor Prince," she went on. "It's been so long since he had a treat. There was Uncle William, of course, and a person who came collecting for the blind, but since then only a few pet guinea pigs and rabbits."

The cat's tail swished to and fro.

"And he's been such a good boy, haven't you, Prince. See—mother's found you this nice girlie, all for yourself."

It felt as though Miss Wigan was tying her hair in a knot over one of the bars. Each single hair seemed to have its own pain centre. To reduce the torment, Susan pushed her head up against the top of the cage. With her neck

127

stretched to its utmost, and held rigid, she could just turn her eyes up to Miss Wigan's mad grey face. It was smiling now, with a sort of terrible benevolence.

"You just keep still, dear," said Miss Wigan, "and it'll all be over in a tick."

Susan couldn't move. She shut her eyes. It wasn't true. It wasn't happening. She smelt that fearsome circus smell. She heard the key in the padlock.

She thought through her panic: *a witch—oh, if only, if only that were all* . . .

Then the door of the cage was opening, and the cat was crouching, it eyes pure yellow evil, its brown teeth wet and bubbling with saliva.

"You'll hardly feel a thing, dear," Miss Wigan said kindly. "He always goes straight for the throat."